To Anthony
"Take care"

THE DEATH
SPREE

J. D. Weisberg

ISBN: 151687126X
ISBN 13: 9781516871261
Library of Congress Control Number: 2015917269
CreateSpace Independent Publishing Platform
North Charleston, South Carolina

*A dying man needs to die, as a sleepy man
needs to sleep, and there comes a time when
it is wrong, as well as useless, to resist.*

—*Stewart Alsop*

CONTENTS

Prologue   vii

1 In the Beginning   1
2 Legends   15
3 Woods   29
4 Killer   44
5 Fact or Fiction   52
6 Runners   62
7 The Ideal   70
8 Occurrences   87
9 Upon Arrival   100
10 The Extravaganza   115
11 Danger, Danger   123
12 Whatever Happens…Happens   138
13 She's Not There   142
14 The Clock Ticks   150
15 Spirits Taking Off   157
16 Over and Over   165
17 As Darkness Closes In   167

18 Phantasmagoria   175
19 It Can't Be…   179
20 Up and Down   188

About the Author   195

PROLOGUE

It was a matter not of *how* cold it was but of *why*. The air was normally cold enough to produce frost but not quite as bone-chilling as it got during the winter of 1952. It was an unusual winter. Maybe not to all the residents of Charleston, West Virginia, but one boy was about to become unbalanced, and his disappearance would fuel fear in the town for decades. There were rumors—that he'd gone too far, that something like a wild animal had killed him, that he'd wanted to get away from life in general.

But there were also rumors that someone—a person, human, flesh and blood—had killed the boy. He had been acting strangely. According to eyewitnesses, his behavior began to get worse as the days went on, until one day he vanished and never came back. But the boy's friend claimed to officers that the last conversation they'd had was completely natural. There were, however, a few clues as to where he might have gone. But the little evidence they did have couldn't prove any of the rumors true or false.

In the decades following his disappearance, murders began to take place every couple of years—brutal, savage murders that were splashed across newspapers by way of lurid headlines. But the murders weren't the only events. Vandalism and arson were common, and the cases were never closed; whoever committed the acts was either still at large or dead. Periods of time would pass, and everyone would forget what had happened. Then the horrific events would kick back up, paralyzing everyone with fear.

The killer targeted no one in particular, but the crimes seemed full of aggression and vengeance. There were no survivors—no one who could get away in time, no one who could evade the killer and live to tell the tale.

By 1976 the problem had become bad enough that the police ordered people to stay in their homes after seven o'clock and advised adults always to escort children. The panic and the fear gave way to paranoia. That same year, the killings stopped. Each year that followed brought worry, though before long it appeared the killings had stopped for good. But they remained fresh in the public mind.

Teenagers in the area began to twist the stories of the murders into their own little scenarios. Legends. That is what the stories evolved into, and soon they spread like wildfire. And who else but the missing boy to use as a potential killer? People began fearing that the missing boy was indeed the murderer, despite that it was only an exaggeration of fact. What a legacy.

So a long-missing child was publicly condemned. His school even threatened to destroy all copies of the yearbooks he was in, claiming the boy had soiled the school's supposed prestige. But why would the boy go missing just to kill? That was the most solid argument against prosecutors who wanted to find the boy and convict him. Therefore, the mystery continued: the disappearance of Ray Kuiper—if it was a disappearance at all.

Legends. They can grow from anything, but sometimes they are taken too seriously. And so the story begins.

1

IN THE BEGINNING

Friday, March 10, 1980—Charleston, West Virginia

Tim Ridges woke up slowly and then moaned as he stumbled over to the calendar by his desk. He held his eyes shut briefly and then looked up. He paused for a second. A vast number of emotions ran though him at that moment, one of which he couldn't identify. It was a mixture of lust, happiness, and his teenage hormones.

He knew a lot of things that might fix his confusion, but he prayed only for one. He stared at the calendar for mere moments. A smile formed on his face as his eyes scanned the date on the calendar. Were his eyes lying to him? Was this the truth? The day for which he'd been readying himself, at first begrudgingly, since he first opened his sleepy eyes was in fact the last day before spring break—and not just any spring break.

It was the spring break of his senior year. The calendar said it was March 10. That date meant nothing to most people, but to Tim it meant freedom. His mother had told him five years ago that during the spring break of his senior year, he could leave the house for the whole week with his friends. He had waited long enough; it was his week to go crazy and get wasted.

Tim opened the door and flew down the hallway to be the first one in the bathroom. It was six in the morning, and his parents would bombard the bathroom door at any second demanding he get out.

His father, Albert, was balding, old—midforties—and calm and collected. His mother, Lorraine, was more uptight. She wore her chestnut hair flipped up, and her deep-brown eyes were always looking for trouble. Tim ran into the bathroom, shut the door, and turned the water on. Normally it took three minutes for the hot water to come on because he was usually the last one to take a shower, but today he waited ten minutes.

He slowly undressed from his red-and-yellow-checkered pajamas and stepped into the shower, letting the warm water massage his skin. Fifteen minutes later, fog was the only thing he could see. Tim felt himself slowly fall into a trance just before his mother banged on the door, nearly making him slip in the shower.

"You'd better get out of there!" Her loud, angry voice echoed off the walls of the bathroom.

"Almost done!" Tim's voice sounded scratchy; these were the first words he'd said all morning. He emitted a heavy sigh as he reluctantly cut the water off.

"Get out!" his mother screamed.

"Calm down, Lorraine!" His father's deep voice was a rumble in his ears.

"No, Albert! He needs to get out."

Should I do this? Face the wrath of my mother this early? He rolled his eyes and then opened the door. His mother was waiting for him, her hands tightened to fists on her hips. One of her feet was tapping impatiently on the floor. She grabbed his arm and pushed him down the hall.

"You be dressed and down for breakfast in five minutes." Tim's mother shoved him into his room and slammed the door.

Tim looked around his bedroom—clothes on the floor, posters hiding his blue walls, brown wooden flooring. He sat down on his bed and stared at the walls. Today was the last day of school for the time being. Spring break with his friends down at a lake house was the event he had been waiting for since he'd begun his high-school life.

His friend Alan had made good on his promise and taken his family's lake house off his parents' hands. He got them to trust him; that's all he needed. Tim went over to his walk-in closet and pulled out the simple outfit that everyone knew him for: a tie-dyed shirt (red, orange, and yellow), semitorn jeans, and some big floppy gray sneakers. He then made his way to the dresser by his bed, opening the top drawer and pulling out a glasses case. Tim put on his big thick-rimmed glasses, took his car keys, exited his room, and headed down the spiral stairwell. He mentally counted the things he wouldn't miss this week, like his family, his bedroom, and his old TV. Tim entered the kitchen, where his parents waited for him at the table. A bowl of cereal and a glass of orange juice sat before him.

Cereal? Again? He took a deep breath and sat down.

"OK." His mother began slowly. "You are going to the lake house with your friends; we've settled that. But because you're still a minor, we just want to go over some rules with you."

"First—" His father cleared his throat.

"First," Tim interrupted, looking around the kitchen and then back at his parents. "I want to let you know Veronica and I will not have sex."

"Oh." His father covered his ears dryly yet jokingly.

"We'll take your word for it, Tim," his mother stated monotonously.

Tim smiled but wondered what his mother meant by that. There's no way she knew about what he and Veronica did when they were alone, was there? Either way, Veronica was his girlfriend of two years; of course they would be having sex. "Second, can I borrow your credit card?"

"No beer," his mother clarified, trying to avoid Tim's statement. "Beer is not good for your body."

"Beer is refreshing," his father said, uncovering his ears and folding his hands. "But no beer for you. You're seventeen."

"Which is why I should be able to have freedom," Tim replied.

Tim's mother breathed in silently. She often became frustrated with his wise remarks. She'd been dealing with them since Tim became a teenager. "You can have my credit card, but I will make sure you have a budget of about fifty dollars."

"Good; that should be enough to buy me booze," Tim said. He took a sip of his orange juice.

"Find someone to buy it for you first," his father said.

"I have my ways." Tim laughed.

As Tim continued to laugh, he failed to notice Lorraine growing more and more frustrated. She managed to keep her cool, though she gave her son and husband annoyed glares. "If I find out you had beer, I will make sure you are grounded for the rest of your life," she said.

"I'm going to college next year, so it won't matter," Tim said.

"If you can get in," his father whispered.

Tim's mother rose from her seat. She wouldn't win this conversation. "We'll finish this when you come home." She took his bowl of untouched cereal and dumped it in the sink.

"Fine." Tim stood up and grabbed his book bag lying on the counter. It was green and torn; he had owned it since the ninth grade and never bothered to get a new one. He opened the front door and strolled outside.

Gray skies covered the town. Tim felt the humidity on his skin, and he loved it. He went over to a big green bush a couple of feet from the door and found a blue skateboard nestled under it. The skateboard belonged to his best friend, Steve Waisner.

Tim grabbed the board and moved on to his 1979 Pontiac Trans Am—solid black with a gold firebird on the hood. He'd gotten it the year before. His mother hadn't wanted him to have it, preferring to hand down her old 1965 Oldsmobile 442, but his dad had gotten the car for him anyway. Tim opened the front door and threw the skateboard into the gray-upholstered backseat.

He got in the car and closed the door. He sat still for a second, thinking about the conversation he'd just had with his parents. Tim understood they were only looking out for him, but it came off more like hassling. He put the key in the ignition, and the Trans Am backed out of the driveway and sped down the road.

Tim drove over to Steve's place, a cream-colored house conveniently located down the block. He honked the horn, and Steve immediately opened the front door and ran over to the car, tightly holding a precalculus textbook.

Steve had hazel eyes and jet-black hair in a shaggy mop-top cut that went down to the center of his neck. He wore a long-sleeved red shirt with blue bell-bottoms and boat shoes. Steve expressed a very nonchalant attitude toward life and was the most levelheaded in their group of friends. Despite this, Steve had found himself in bad situations more than once.

"Hey, man!" Steve smiled as he jumped in. "Veronica, Rod, and Alan are going to meet us at school."

"Sounds good," Tim said, driving away. "And can you believe my parents think Veronica and I are having sex?"

Steve looked over at his friend and grinned. "Can you believe it's true?" He laughed as Tim smiled and rolled his eyes.

"Well, it's sad they don't trust me." Tim's smile faded into a frown as he thought about the conversation with his parents.

"I wouldn't trust you."

"That's because you get me. My dead cat understood me better than my parents do."

"Well, you also spent a bunch of time with Spiffy. Damn shame he passed."

"My father buried him alive." Tim stopped in front of a big gray mansion—Elizabeth's house.

Elizabeth Carlough was a stunningly gorgeous girl with shoulder-length brown hair and glossy teal eyes—the shade of Brooke Shields's eyes. She was a classic rich beauty. Her parents were among the wealthiest in Charleston, and Liz, as she liked to be called, proudly flaunted it all the time. A year younger than the rest of the core group, Liz was the girlfriend of Rod Grandt, one of Steve and Tim's closest friends.

"Ugh!" Steve exclaimed, aggravated, as he saw which house Tim had pulled up to. "Do we have to pick up Liz?"

"We don't *have* to, but Rod insists somebody do it. He can't, because her father hates him."

"Still, why can't Alan or Veronica get her?" Steve moaned.

Liz rushed outside wearing a pastel-yellow sundress and tan heels and carrying a big hobo bag over her shoulder. Her clothes surprised Tim and Steve, as she usually dressed in flashy and extravagant outfits even though they were only heading to school.

"Guys!" The two guys cringed as they heard her high-pitched voice.

"Back." Tim pointed to the backseat.

Steve got out of the car so Liz could slide into the backseat. Everyone liked Tim's car, but the two-door setting proved to be bothersome.

As Liz climbed in, the smell of rich perfume filled the air. The boys immediately rolled down their windows. Tim would have held his breath all the way to school if he could.

"Where are we going now?" Liz bounced up and down.

"Stop jumping!" Steve rolled his eyes. "Richie's place."

"Fun, fun, fun!" Liz exclaimed.

"I'm excited for the lake house," Steve said to Tim, trying to ignore Liz.

"I know, right?" Liz butted in. "How did Alan score this?"

"Easy. Alan got his parents to trust him with the lake house," Tim said. "I can't believe it, but I'm glad he did."

"Besides, our spring break will be filled with beer, sex, and everything in between." Steve smiled, satisfied at his own comment.

"We can't pick up Rod?" Liz leaned in toward Tim before he could respond to Steve.

"Your boyfriend has a car—that old black station wagon."

"You could've at least *offered* to pick him up." Liz crossed her arms and pouted.

It was times like this Tim and Steve tried very hard not to do something they'd regret in the long run.

The rest of the drive was silent until the car pulled up to a small green house with a large front lawn. Tim honked the horn, and Richie Warson stepped out.

"Hey, everyone!" Richie ran over to the car. He carried three textbooks in his arms—AP physics, AP psychology, and AP trigonometry. Steve opened the door for him, and Richie slid past Liz and sat down, crossing his legs.

Richie wore a white T-shirt, denim pants, and boat shoes. He had wavy black hair and dark eyes. He still had a slender lacrosse player's build even though his parents had forced him to quit the team. They wanted him to focus on his studies so he could someday go to medical school. Despite the setbacks—and the fact that he was barely passing any of his AP classes—Richie always had smart-aleck grin on his face to show nothing brought him down.

"Pretty chill, man," Tim said as he waited for Steve to close the door before driving off again.

"What?" Liz asked.

"I'm talking about Richie's outfit," said Tim, looking at Richie in the rearview mirror. "It seems like everyone's wearing boat shoes but me."

"Didn't get the memo?" Richie questioned. He saw the skateboard leaning against his door and handed it to Steve, who thanked him.

"I'm so excited for the lake house!" Liz jumped up and down, again blocking out the conversations among the guys.

"Stop jumping!" Tim and Steve shouted. The two groaned and exhaled audibly in unison.

"I'm not gonna lie—so am I." Richie put an arm around Liz's shoulder. "Oh, did you guys know tonight is the annual sleepover in the school?"

"So?" Tim pulled up to a big redbrick building. School. He parked the car in the student parking lot.

"We need to go!" Richie exclaimed. "We gotta keep the coolness of school events as we usually do. Therefore, we are going."

"Is that final?" Tim asked, unlocking the doors.

"Everything I say is final," Richie replied.

The entire group exited the car. They all stood together for a couple of minutes, leaning on the trunk, waiting for the rest of their friends to meet them. The roar of an engine sounded as an old black station wagon took the parking space next to the group.

"Rod!" Liz jumped up and down, greeting her boyfriend as he hopped out of the car to kiss her passionately.

"Again with the jumping?" Steve whispered to Tim. They both began walking away.

"Guys, are you waiting for Alan?" Rod yelled as Liz clung to him. Other students stared.

"Alan and Veronica will meet us later," Steve answered as he waved them away.

"Word," Tim added as he and Steve made their way into the building.

The building was cold, old, and—frankly—depressing. From the faded-blue lockers to the dirty white tile, everything was falling apart in Franklin Pierce High School. Luckily Tim and his friends were all seniors, so this would be their last year sulking around the halls.

"I think I'm finally getting used to the fact that we're almost out of here," Tim said, checking out the posters for the basketball game from the week before.

They bypassed classrooms, sometimes glancing inside to say hello to acquaintances. They stopped in front of a big glass door that led out to the courtyard. The Spot, as the students called it, had begun filling up with people.

"I agree. Strange to think we've been here for four years now." Steve leaned against the wall, looking outside at the people lounging about. "Hell, I still remember the first day of freshman year."

Richie, Liz, and Rod soon appeared out of the hallway. Rod had an arm wrapped around Liz's waist. He looked up at the gray ceiling in disgust.

Rod Grandt had wavy, feathered dark-brown hair and dark-emerald eyes. He wore a navy-blue polo, dark denim jeans, and white Nikes. A rather popular guy around Franklin Pierce High, Rod didn't play sports or take part in school events, but people liked him because of his laid-back approach to life. At least that's how the other guys around school saw him. The girls instead lusted after his handsome appearance.

"Has Alan come yet?" Tim asked, looking around the hallway. Students had started filling the halls.

"Haven't seen him. But he should be here soon. His Gremlin isn't the most reliable vehicle in the world." Rod chuckled. "Oh, and Richie told me we're spending the night in the school this evening. Also, we're apparently meeting at Liz's. Is that so?"

"Sounds decent," said a voice from behind.

Tim smiled as his girlfriend appeared. Veronica Leeds. A girl with strikingly bold green-blue eyes; olive-colored skin; wild, somewhat wavy black hair that hung to her torso; and perfect soft lips. She wore a long-sleeved gray button-down shirt, worn jeans, and black Converses. Pleasant and outgoing, with a mind sharper than a blade, she was easily the best girl in the school—and she was all his. Veronica wrapped her arms around his neck and kissed him on the lips.

"Ew." Steve put his hands over his eyes.

"Get over it." Tim pushed Steve's hands away and smiled at him. He then turned back to Veronica, holding her waist. "Well, now you know—we're spending the night at the school, going to the lake house tomorrow, and then staying there all week. We'll meet at Liz's house tonight by...let's say six. Got it?"

"I sure do." Veronica nodded. "And can you believe just two more months here and we'll be gone?" she said happily.

As the first bell chimed, the group was about to go their separate ways when another voice stopped them in their tracks.

"All the things I've put myself through, and I'm still waiting for the time when you guys are gonna thank me."

Everyone turned around and smiled. Alan Prelle stood there grinning. Called an impulsive jokester by the teachers (and Tim's parents), Alan differed from the usual stereotype, as he knew not to push boundaries too far but still made others laugh.

Alan had brown eyes and short ash-brown hair in a slight pompadour style that went down to his upper neck. He wore a red polo and jeans, along with a blue baseball cap. Alan called it his lucky cap, and he had been wearing it since the eighth grade. His grandfather had given it to him shortly before he passed away, and Alan wore the cap in his honor.

"Thank you, Alan!" everyone shouted.

"No problem, guys." Alan grinned. "All you gotta do is get your parents to trust you."

"Alan, we're all spending the night at the school. You wanna stay?" Rod asked.

"Hell yeah!" Alan replied as he high-fived Rod.

"Cool. We're meeting at my place at six, OK?" Liz beamed.

"Gotcha." Alan snapped his fingers. The warning bell rang.

"This will be awesome." Liz jumped up and down even more excitedly than usual.

"Stop jumping, dammit!" Veronica yelled. Veronica shared Tim and Steve's annoyance toward Liz. Like Tim, Veronica thought Liz craved attention everywhere and anywhere.

"Thank you!" everyone remarked—excluding Liz and Rod.

Then they went to class. Tim dragged his feet all the way to first period. He took his seat in the middle of the classroom and conversed with some acquaintances. When the final bell rang, however, Tim zoned out, daydreaming about Veronica, the lake house, and his nights alone.

The bell for lunch chimed. Tim sat in his third-period class, US government, staring at the wall. His last classes—precalculus and marine science—had been a blur. Tim grabbed his books and rushed out of the classroom, bypassing a crowd of friends and a group of girls calling his name.

The smell of roasted chicken filled the small warm lunchroom. He skipped getting lunch and sat down at the center table. His friends followed soon after. They claimed that table because, as the center of the school's social life, they felt they deserved it.

"Tonight I have legends to tell you guys." Alan shoved mashed potatoes into his mouth.

"Cool." Liz pulled a mirror out of her handbag and primped. "I can't help but say it again: I am excited."

Rod put his arm around Liz, and she put her hand on his. Rod's head drooped slightly; he seemed tired.

"Don't get too scared by my stories before we come here, though." Alan laughed. "I think Liz or Steve will get scared first."

"In your dreams, Alan." Steve fiddled with his hair. "If anything, you will get scared by your own stories."

"I will get scared," Liz admitted.

"It's all right; I doubt I'll get scared, though." Richie sat down next to Alan and took a bite of the roasted chicken. He had been flirting with a few girls at another table.

"You guys are stupid." Tim stared into space, not really giving second thought to his friends. Veronica reached for his hand, but he pulled away. "Besides," he continued, "this school event is minor compared to what is to come at the lake house." He kissed Veronica on the cheek, and she blushed.

"The lake house is going to be a blast! I get away from my overprotective parents," Liz said, pausing for a second to apply lip gloss. "They want me to get with Stan Alewine—y'know, the guy whose family owns, like, everything in town." She paused again. "Anyway, his family is, like, superrich, and so is mine, and they think that if we can combine our net funds, we can be the richest family in this region."

"That's bogue. Rod and you look good together." Steve crossed his arms and took another sip of his fruit punch.

"That's what I'm trying to tell them, but Father thinks Rod is a hood." Liz pouted.

Rod just shrugged. He had been having problems with Liz's father for the entire relationship. Liz's father didn't care for the others either. Her mother, however, at least treated each kid with respect. But Tim knew Rod really wanted *both* of his girlfriend's parents to like him.

"West Virginia has its fair share of riches." Veronica rolled her eyes. "But if anything, you don't need to be cockier than you already are."

"I am not cocky!"

"Easy, Liz," Rod said. Tim noticed Rod's eyes were bloodshot, and his face seemed red.

"What's wrong, Rod?" Veronica asked before Tim could.

"Nothing. Just tired, I guess." Rod sighed.

"Of hearing Liz's voice. I know that has to be it! Because you like it when she jumps." Steve laughed. "Am I wrong, guys?"

"You're right. Rod, you fantasize!" Tim shouted.

"You undress her with your eyes." Richie grinned.

"And you like it," Alan added.

The group all laughed as Liz groaned. Ever since she began dating Rod, she'd put up with the constant antics of his friends. Though accustomed to it, she obviously still hated it. A teacher came by to hush them, but Tim shooed him off.

"Anyway, my mom thinks Tim and I are perfect together," Veronica said. She and Tim smiled at each other.

"You are," Alan admitted. "You guys look amazing together."

"Almost better than my parents did together." Steve crossed his arms again. "Note the word 'did,' because now they are old sags."

"Ha!" Tim laughed. "Well, at least your mom is chill. My mom still acts like she has a stick up her ass."

"Speaking of parents, mine have finally learned how to trust me after that party I threw freshman year." Alan grinned.

Alan's party of December 1976 was legendary. Being a freshman, Alan hadn't been sure how many people would show up at his party besides his pals. With his parents out of town for the week, he'd wanted to build at least some credit around the school. But word of mouth made it seem like Alan was a party master, and when he opened his front door that night, history ran its course.

"No one's thrown a party like that since." Veronica smiled. "Not that anything could top it."

"Talk about grounded for almost all of ninth grade," Alan said.

"Could be worse." Tim shrugged. "And besides, everyone from our district went to your house. Even much older kids."

"That's because when you're Alan Prelle, anything can happen," said Rod, more faintly this time. The group tried to laugh at the comment. Rod was still smiling but definitely more wearily.

"So about the house," Liz chimed in, perking up and holding her boyfriend closer. "Tell me more."

"It is a three-story, sky-blue-colored beauty. It has four bedrooms—one king-size, one bunk, and two queen-size," Alan told the rest of the group. "I'll tell you all the sleeping arrangements when we get there, but everyone knows who's rooming together already, right?" Alan nudged Tim's shoulder a few times, causing Tim to jokingly shove him lightly. Veronica shook her head, smiling at Alan.

"Are there any neighbors by us?" Rod asked.

"No, it's just a house in the woods."

"The woods?" Liz shouted. Everyone in the lunchroom looked at her.

A teacher gave the group the signal to be quiet, and they were silent for a few moments. As the other students went back to what they were doing, the group laughed—everyone but Liz, who was still in a state of fear, and Rod.

"Quiet down, babe. There is nothing wrong with that, OK?" Rod sounded irritated, somewhat stern. Tim looked at Veronica, who raised her eyebrows in shock. This wasn't like Rod—not at all.

"Rod, what's got you all upset?" Liz got concerned as she motioned for Rod to lie down on her lap.

Rod's eyes were still bloodshot, though his face finally lost the red hue that had previously flushed it. He sighed and laid his head on his girlfriend's lap. "I don't know. I'm sorry I got all mad at you, babe. You did nothing."

Liz ran her fingers through his hair, mouthing, "I understand" to him.

"Take a chill." Steve rolled his eyes. "When you're angry, you can be worse than Elizabeth when she jumps."

"I like jumping." Liz jumped up and down eagerly as everyone complained. Steve grabbed his fruit punch, pretending to take aim at Liz.

Tim looked at Rod, head still resting on Liz's bouncing lap and looking up. Everything about his facial expression said that he wanted more, but his body language asked for less.

"Over here!" Alan called the custodian over to pick up their garbage as he finished his milk.

"I love being the center of everyone's attention." Liz smiled as she stopped jumping.

"Because you're a conceited airhead," Veronica added. "Besides, what's the worst that could happen when you're popular, aside from being hated?"

"I love being hated," Alan said.

"Me too," everyone agreed.

2

LEGENDS

Tim sat down quietly at his kitchen table. Other than meeting with his friends, eating lunch, and driving home, the memory of school today was nothing but a haze. It was exactly 5:08 p.m., and Tim tapped his foot against the tile, anxiously waiting to get out of the house already. His parents came downstairs in the same clothes they'd greeted him in that morning. Tim was initially surprised they hadn't gone to work, but he remembered they had planned to take time off while he was away. His father worked for the IRS as a tax collector, while his mother worked as a pharmacist for the local drugstore.

"Timothy." His mother sat down next to him and his father in front of him.

"Yes, Mother?"

"I want you to understand our rules." She was speaking too softly, too innocently.

"Yeah, yeah, yeah. No beer, no sex. I understand," Tim grumbled.

"That's not it," his father added. "We want you to be safe."

"Dad, what could possibly go wrong at a lake house in the woods?" Tim asked, smiling at his own stupid statement.

"Please," his mother begged. "I will give you fifty dollars—no need for my card. Just do not spend it on booze."

"You have my word." Tim slouched in his chair and looked at the clock. It was 5:10 p.m.

"And if you do have sex, be safe, OK?" Albert crossed his hands.

"Yes, Father." Tim sat back up and copied his father's body language. He crossed his arms and gave a half smile.

"We aren't joking, Tim. Please be safe." His mother's voice went up.

Tim stared at his mother. He couldn't believe she, of all people, had said that to him. He'd expected her to give his father an irritated scowl, but instead she'd answered that way? Tim buried his face into his hands, trying to block out the image of Veronica pregnant and him paying child support.

"Little Timmy is growing up." His father patted him on the back. "That's all we have to tell you, Son."

"Yeah, thanks, Dad," Tim mumbled, trying to mask his aggravation at being called Timmy. He wasn't a little kid anymore, and being called that made him feel as though he were being babied. He dragged his body upstairs to his room.

The mess of his room made him feel more at home. Tim kicked off his gray shoes and jumped on his bed, not hesitating to close his eyes. Before he fell into a trance, he thought about things that might go wrong, one being Rod falling asleep before they could leave. And the other—the sound of the phone ringing interrupted his thoughts. Tim groaned, but he didn't get off his bed. He was too comfortable at the moment. Then his mother's voice resonated from downstairs.

"Tim, get the phone!" she yelled.

Annoyed, Tim reluctantly raised himself and made his way over to the rotary phone on his dresser. He held the handset loosely to his ear.

"Hello?" he sighed.

"Good, you're on," his mother said before she hung up.

"Talk to me," Tim said.

"Tim? Tim, is this you?" He recognized the voice. Jacqueline Grandt, Rod's mother. His heart skipped a beat.

"Yeah, it is, Mrs. Grandt. What happened?"

"Rod was in a car accident! He fell asleep at the wheel."

"Oh my gosh!" Tim's mother cut in. "Is he OK?" Tim wondered why she had picked up the phone again.

"Yes, he's fine," Mrs. Grandt replied, to Tim's relief. "No serious injuries. But I don't think he's able to go to that sleepover the school is holding tonight."

"Yes I can, Mom!" Rod's anxious voice rang in the background. "Tim can drive me."

"Honey, you fell asleep at the wheel!" Mrs. Grandt exclaimed.

"And I only hit a tree near our house. I'm fine!" Rod called.

"I can drive him," Tim said, trying hard not to laugh at Rod's comment of having *only* hit a tree.

"He sounds a bit too tired to go, Tim." Rod's mother tried to sound happy, ignoring her son's yelling in the background.

"It's a sleepover at the school! If I'm tired, then I go to bed there! Take it into consideration!" Rod shouted.

Tim heard a loud slam over the other line.

"Oh, Rod!" Mrs. Grandt said and then hung up the phone.

A few moments of awkward silence passed between Tim and his mother before she finally said, "You can get off the phone now."

Tim hung up, jumped on his bed, and began to dream.

Tim's eyes fluttered open at exactly 6:00 p.m. Veronica stood over him, breathing heavily. Her scent of roses filled the air, and he grabbed her waist, pulling his girlfriend underneath him.

"How did you get in?" He tried making his voice as seductive as possible.

"The front door. Your mom let me in. What happened with Rod?"

"How did you find out?"

"Rod's mom called Liz, who called Richie, who called Alan, who called Steve, who called me."

"Wow. Word gets around fast." Tim smiled. He leaned closer and kissed her soft neck. Veronica's eyes closed, and she began to tremble. Whenever Tim kissed her neck, she lost her train of thought. In other words, neck kisses turned her on. Veronica began to moan softly, which encouraged Tim to continue.

"No." She pulled away, albeit reluctantly. "Your parents are still home. You know they wouldn't let me in your room with your door closed. I came because I'm picking you up, remember?"

"Doesn't stop you from sneaking in late at night sometimes." Tim smirked. "And yeah, I can't. I kind of promised to take Rod."

"I can take Rod too."

"Yeah, but..." Tim tried to make an excuse; he didn't want his girlfriend driving him. It would make him seem weak in his eyes.

"Please," she begged.

Tim said nothing, and Veronica saw her boyfriend was still trying to make up his mind. She gave him a quick kiss to settle it for him. Veronica could always make her boyfriend give in, but she didn't abuse that privilege...too often.

"Fine." Tim jumped off his bed and grabbed a pair of sweatpants and his favorite white shirt off his bed frame before throwing his gray shoes back on.

"Let's go!" Veronica jumped up and opened the door.

The two walked down the stairs. Tim's mother and father were watching *Titanic*, starring Clifton Webb and Barbara Stanwyck, and snuggling on the couch. The lights were off, and popcorn was the only thing Tim could smell. He rolled his eyes as he and Veronica made it out of the house trying not to disturb his parents.

"This is gonna be killer!" Tim said, running over to Veronica's pale-yellow 1979 Volvo wagon.

"For sure." Veronica jumped in the driver's side as Tim got in the passenger's.

"You remember where he lives, right?" Tim asked.

"Of course I do," Veronica stated. "Richie, Alan, and Steve should be at Liz's house already." She pulled out of the driveway.

"The sleepover starts at eight and ends at nine tomorrow morning," Tim said. "I say we meet about nine thirty at my place, get some breakfast, chill at one of our houses, at twelve get some lunch, and then at about four, we can leave for the lake house."

"Seems a little late."

"Yes, but when the sun sets, it's more romantic for some of the things Rod and I have planned for you and Liz." Tim put his hand on Veronica's thigh.

"What about Richie and Alan?" Veronica laughed, running her fingers across his hand.

"They can love each other."

Veronica laughed more. She returned her hand to the wheel. "Oh, is Steve bringing that girl he's been talking to? He mentioned her before I left to get you."

"What do you mean?" Tim looked at Veronica. "What girl?"

"You know, to the sleepover."

Tim had to think for a moment. Veronica's comment didn't help him any. "Wait, you mean his lab partner, Tammy Heston?"

"Yeah, Tammy!" Veronica nodded. "I don't like her."

Tim and Veronica shared a laugh as they entered Rod's lavish, tree-filled neighborhood.

"Yeah. I thought Liz was annoying, but Tammy's worse," Tim said.

"I can't stand her, plan and simple," Veronica stated

They pulled up to a sidewalk next to a two-story brick house with steel trim around the windows. Even more trees covered the entrance, and a large black gate stared at them from the front of the house.

"Steve's coming to Liz's first, right?" Tim asked.

"Of course. Let's go." She unlocked the doors, and they both jumped out of the car.

"Wait. Steve told me a few days ago he wanted Tammy to come to the lake house with us. She said she couldn't," Tim commented.

"That's OK." Veronica chuckled. "Less of us having to put up with her."

"True, but knowing Steve, I don't think he and Tammy are gonna be hanging around us much during the sleepover."

"Why do you say that?"

"Steve's probably planning to have sex with her somewhere on the grounds."

"Sounds like Steve. Who in the school hasn't he slept with?" Veronica joked, smiling at Tim as they walked. Tim slipped his hand into hers.

"He isn't that bad of guy," Tim whispered, looking at Veronica as they both walked up to the buzzer at the gate. "Gosh…rich people."

Tim hadn't been to Rod's house in nearly a year, but his reaction was always the same upon arriving at the gate. For friends who used to be really close as children, Tim hardly saw Rod outside of school nowadays unless the group got together someplace around town. The last time he'd hung out solely with Rod was the beginning of freshman year.

"You're telling me." Veronica rolled her eyes. "Did his mom even say yes to this?"

"Well, I'm not sure…but he did. Hell, I'm not even sure he's home."

"Hello?" Mrs. Grandt's voice came through the speaker attached to the buzzer.

"Oh, hello, Mrs. Grandt." Veronica's voice was suddenly higher and preppier. Tim shook his head in amusement.

"Veronica, is that you, darling? Hold on one second!" The gate opened all the way. "Please come in!" Veronica shrugged, and Tim followed her past the gate.

Neat red roses adorned the freshly cut lawn going up to the front porch. Tim and Veronica walked up a spotted tile pathway to the glass door. Rod leaned his back against it from the inside. Tim knocked lightly, and Rod turned to them.

"Hey, bro," Tim said as Rod opened the door.

"Hey, Tim, Veronica."

"Rod." Veronica smiled.

"Bye, honey!" his mother called from inside.

Rod waved at his mother as he continued out to the Volvo wagon. He didn't bother turning to her.

"We'll take good care of him, Mrs. Grandt," Tim reassured her.

"And don't worry; I think he just needs to get out of the house for the time being," Veronica added. She said good-bye to Mrs. Grandt as she closed the door.

Rod claimed the passenger's side as Veronica jumped in the driver's seat, forcing Tim to get in the backseat.

"So, what's going on, Rod?" Tim broke the short silence as Veronica drove out of Rod's neighborhood.

"Same old, same old." Rod rested his head against the window as he stared off into the darkening sky.

"Come on, man." Tim shifted to the center of the car and looked at Rod.

"Look. It's nothing, Tim!" Rod shouted, startling Veronica and, to some extent, Tim. "It's just nothing at all." He sighed.

"You can tell us, Rod. You can tell us anything," Veronica responded, keeping her eyes on the road. "Is Liz pregnant or something?"

"No." Rod shook his head.

"Then what's going?" Tim continued.

"Tim, please stop being so damn persistent. Nothing is happening!" Rod nearly jumped out of his seat as he turned toward Tim.

Strange. Rod never acted this way. Something had to be going on, and whatever it was, it was eating at him. And Tim didn't like it. Here they were giving Rod a ride, and this is how he decided to treat them? Tim understood that maybe he shouldn't have been pestering his friend, but he also didn't like getting screamed at. That triggered his temper.

"Stop the car, Veronica," Tim demanded.

"What?" Veronica looked at Rod.

"Stop the damn car!" Tim shouted as she hit the brakes, causing the car to jolt and stop short.

Tim hated having to shout at his girlfriend, but he was getting aggravated, and sparks flew when he got that way. They stopped in the middle of an abandoned dirt road, a shortcut that led to Liz's place.

"Get the hell out, Rod. You want me to leave you alone? Then you can just get out!"

"Fine, asshole." Rod unlocked his door and opened it a tad.

"Rod, no." Veronica turned to him. "We're almost at Liz's. Let's settle this," she begged.

Rod stepped out of the car for a second before zipping back into his seat, closing the door, and locking it as soon as possible. He looked at Tim and Veronica, stunned. Tim didn't know how to react.

"Did you see that?" Rod said, his eyes widening.

"What?" Tim looked out the window.

"I could've sworn I just saw a figure appear by the car."

"Yeah. Me too." Veronica's voice got shallow. "We need to get out of here."

The sun was setting, and darkness loomed.

"What did the figure look like?" Tim asked Rod while Veronica put the car in drive.

"It was dark, and it was holding something sharp—like maybe a knife."

A crow cawed.

"It's unnerving," Rod admitted. He took a deep breath and closed his eyes. "I'm sorry, guys. I guess I should confess before the word gets out. My parents have decided to get a divorce, and it's hard for me right now. I guess I didn't want to talk about it. It's one of those things you never expect to happen, and I figured if I said nothing, I could somehow forget about it."

Tim's and Veronica's attitudes completely turned around. Tim felt guilty for having yelled at his friend; Veronica was sympathetic. Her parents had divorced six years earlier.

"This shortcut's creeping me out too. And I want to apologize, Rod. I honestly can't imagine the stress you must be going through," Tim said.

"Don't apologize, Tim. It's OK. I just wish I knew why this is happening. I think it has to do with money, but I don't know for sure. They won't tell me. Michelle and I are scared. We've heard them arguing at night, and Mom's been insisting she wants full custody. Losing Dad will be like a kick in the face, even if it's just for a few months before I head off to college."

"I am so sorry." Veronica's mouth trembled as her eyes filled with tears.

"As am I. I shouldn't have snapped at you two," Rod admitted.

"Same goes for me," Tim said.

The Volvo wagon made it back to civilization and pulled up to Liz's mansion. The three friends walked up a set of concrete steps toward the door. Tim rang the doorbell, and Liz answered.

"Hey, guys!" Liz beamed.

"Hey, Liz." Tim and Veronica spoke together. They forced smiles and walked inside, moving past her.

Rod put a hand on his girlfriend's hip, kissing her lightly on the lips as he attempted to walk inside with her, but she stopped him in his tracks.

"Rod, sweetie, are you sure you're OK?" Liz asked, her voice full of concern.

"I am, babe. I realized that I just can't be away from you for so long." Rod kissed Liz on the cheek. He didn't want her to worry about him.

"You're so adorable!" Liz jumped up and down.

Veronica and Tim winced as her voice echoed throughout the house. They took seats next to Richie and Steve in the massive living room. Alan walked out of the kitchen.

"I don't tell you this enough, but I love it when you jump," Rod said as he picked up Liz and brought her inside, kicking the door shut.

Rod carried Liz over to the living room, where everyone else lounged around. Golden-yellow paint adorned the walls of the house. Plastic covered the furniture, and the sunset radiated from the windows surrounding the living room. Various old pictures of Liz's family members hung on the walls. The group sat on the couch eating chocolate-chip cookies as Rod and Liz took their seats.

"Steve, talk to me about Tammy again," Tim said.

"Well, what do you want to know, buddy?" Steve smiled.

"Your plans with her, man."

"Easy; we're gonna sneak away from the rest of you guys after about thirty minutes of hanging out. I don't know where we'll go, but we'll figure something out. And wherever we go, what happens next is common knowledge." Steve grinned widely.

Alan and Richie clapped in approval. Steve's grin grew even larger, but Veronica seemed skeptical. "And just how do you plan on finding an open room in the school?" she asked.

"Tammy told me she has her ways," Steve smirked.

"Sleeping with the janitor, no doubt," Liz mumbled under her breath.

The rivalry between Liz and Tammy was well known to everyone at the school. Tammy had been one of Liz's closest friends since middle school, but recently the two had stopped hanging out together over some "stupid reason"—that reason being that the two of them had bought the same dress for the winter formal and neither had wanted to return hers to please the other.

"Sounds nice, bro, but why not something more romantic like what Rod and I have planned for Liz and Veronica at the lake house?" Tim asked.

"Because it's Steve, and a romantic is the last thing he is," Alan joked.

The group laughed as Steve shook his head, smiling. Alan had made a point, however. Steve wasn't a very romantic person at all. His preference was to—if he was going to sleep with a girl—just do it.

"What do you have planned?" Liz asked Rod, trying to change the subject.

"Can't say, but it's good," Rod said with a smile.

"I think she's gonna be great," Steve said, switching back to the original topic.

"Does she know you're gonna score with her, hotshot?" Veronica laughed.

"Yeah," Steve replied nonchalantly. "As a matter of fact, she instigated it in physics today." He stopped to glance at Richie. "Regular—not AP, like the brain over here." Richie gave Steve a death stare as he continued. "We were about to mix chemicals, and Tammy tells me she thinks I'm cute. I look at her and just reply back, as casual as can be, that I find her rather—well, sexy. Suddenly she tells me she's been very 'lonely' the past couple of months. While I'm listening, I'm just staring into her eyes, her body language speaking more than her words. I flat out asked her if she was going to the sleepover tonight. She told me that if I'm there, so is she." Steve grinned again.

"Nice, man," Tim said as he high-fived Steve.

Rod stood up from his seat and picked up Alan's glass of milk along with a spoon. He clanged the glass a couple of times to get everyone's attention. "So, I have legends to tell you, and I find it's time for them to be told," he said.

"Whoa, whoa, whoa." Alan stood up as well, grabbing his glass of milk from Rod's hand. "I thought I was gonna tell them."

"I know 'em better." Rod smiled as he whacked the bill of Alan's baseball cap down in front of his eyes and gently pushed him back down.

"Tell them!" Liz jumped up and down.

"Earthquake!" Richie cupped his mouth and bellowed.

Everyone howled with laughter, and Liz scowled at them. Rod too seemed irritated at Richie's remark. Liz walked into the kitchen in a huff. Rod frowned but tried to maintain the mysterious air of the still-untold story.

"Babe, you'll miss the legends," Rod said in a voice that sounded as though a Greek man was trying to speak in a British accent.

"Go on!" Veronica insisted.

"All right." Rod got down to business, taking a seat. "Once there was a kid named Ray Kuiper."

"Ky-pehr?" Steve interrupted. "That's a funny last name."

"Ha, yeah! And what's with the phony French accent?" Richie added, causing everyone to snicker. Liz walked back from the kitchen with a bowl of honeydew melon.

"South African, not French," Rod remarked. "Anyway, Ray Kuiper was this groovy kid—I mean, like, really groovy. But he kinda sorta had a secret."

"What was it?" Liz asked.

Rod put a finger on Liz's lips. "I'm getting there. He went to Franklin Pierce High School in the early fifties. But on one bizarre day, Kuiper went in and never went out."

Richie oohed and aahed to make light of the situation. But no one was ready for the big reveal. Rod stared at the glowing embers from the fireplace behind the television set. The friends all sat on the edges of their seats. *What happened next? Did Ray Kuiper die? Did he disappear?* No one asked these questions aloud. That would have only destroyed the growing excitement.

"They found his body in a chemical wastebasket. The custodians smelled rotted, burned flesh, and they found him...burned alive," Rod said.

"Who killed him?" Steve asked, his face frozen.

"No one knows. Back then they said it was an act of suicide," Rod replied.

"What was his secret?"

"No one knows that either. A message was on the wastebasket, written in blood: 'I have a secret to tell.'"

Tim began to wonder if this was a mere legend or if it was a true story. A lot of legends built themselves from true occurrences, Bloody Mary being the most recognizable case.

"Not true. No way this is true." Liz pulled out a big, slim box from under the couch. It held stories that her parents had kept that were interesting or entertaining or just mentioned their names. Rod said Kuiper went to their high school in the fifties—surely there would be some news articles about the event.

"Are you seriously looking this up, babe?" Rod asked. "Go ahead. You might even find old pictures of his body. This was back in nineteen fifty-two."

Steve hopped off the couch and began to search through the box with Liz. He wanted to know whether this story was a farce. He tossed aside unrelated articles before grabbing a beaten newspaper clipping. His smile faded as he showed it to everyone. Liz scurried back to the couch and grabbed Rod's thigh.

"How do you know about this?" Tim took a bite of a cookie.

"Everyone knows about him. And they think he's coming back to avenge his *murder*—because he didn't kill himself. Or so they say," Rod answered.

"Wicked!" Veronica exclaimed.

"We need to check this out," Alan whispered.

"Maybe Kuiper was the mysterious figure Tim, Rod, and I saw on the way here? We can go back in these woods," Veronica suggested.

Liz had had enough of all this talk about trying to inspect some creepy mystery. She was right about the prediction she'd made during lunch earlier. She was very scared, and she wasn't afraid to admit that fact. "We are all going to die!" she screamed.

"Oh, here we go again." Tim rolled his eyes.

"We're not the Scooby-Doo gang or the Jabberjaw clan," Liz pleaded. "I mean, I guess I'm eager too, but I don't—it's too late. I mean, we can do this when break is over."

"Fun, fun!" Richie clapped his hands, doing a cheap imitation of Liz. "I say we go now. The sleepover begins in two hours, and we could try to find clues while Steve and Tammy get it on." He emphasized the last part.

"And anything that happens will be on the surveillance cameras around the school," Veronica said.

"Who cares?" Steve smiled.

"Another reason we should not go!" Liz yelled. "The sleepover tonight is just going to be scary."

"It's just a legend, Liz!" Tim said. "Chill out."

"Yeah, babe. It's *only* a legend." Rod put his arms around Liz, and everything got silent.

3

WOODS

"These woods are really scary." Liz held on to a flashlight as she and Tim wandered through the woods.

According to the plan, the friends had broken into three groups. Veronica, Alan, Rod, and Richie had all left to go to the school. Steve went to pick up Tammy from her house, while Tim and Liz stayed behind to investigate the mysterious shadow that Rod and Veronica had seen during the ride to Liz's house.

To Liz's chagrin, everyone but her boyfriend had forced her to go along with Tim just for the hell of it. She hated forests, even the woods by her own house, whether it was day or night. To make things worse, Liz had a strong feeling Tim was accompanying her against his will. He didn't want to be there with her. The miserable expression on his face said it all.

"Why are we here, anyway?" Liz continued. "I just got my nails done for the lake house, and the others know I didn't want to be in these woods in the first place. I mean, can you believe the insensitivity of—"

Tim held up his finger irritably. "Why is it you don't know when to shut up?" He said softly.

Tim had changed into his white shirt and sweatpants. Liz wore a periwinkle sweater, black sweatpants, and brown boots. The trees seemed to touch the sky, which seemed to be fading into darkness. Everything appeared calmer, softer, at night.

Liz scoffed. "Well, I don't like you guys either. I'm only 'friends' with you guys because of Rod."

"Go back to your straitlaced rich friends. The others and I are too much for you, and you know that."

"They are not!" Liz glared at Tim.

"Yes they are! You can't do anything but complain and go on and on about how rich you are! If it wasn't for your mother's chocolate truffles, I wouldn't even go over to your house."

Liz clenched her fists and then shoved Tim slightly. "I can go back to hanging with friends who have class—Tammy and all them. I may despise Tammy, but I sure can tolerate her more than you poor scumbags!" Her voice echoed through the forest as all got silent.

The two had lost the trail they'd been on, and now the sound of cracking branches echoed. Liz's flashlight beam continued to shine on their surroundings. She sniffled, wondering why she'd spoken that way. Her parents always told her not to lose her temper over little things. That's what this was.

"Can't believe I said that," Liz whispered, wiping a tear away.

"Why do you like Rod, anyway? He's wrong for you. You guys have nothing in common."

"I—"

"Is it because your parents want you to be with Stan? Is it because you want to go against their will?"

"But—"

"And it's not only because all the girls think he's handsome, right? It'd be pretty damn bad if you were only dating my pal for his looks." He laughed.

"Screw off, Tim. I fucking love Rod!" Liz took all the pent-up anger she'd built over the past months, shoved Tim harder, and then proceeded to hit his back with the flashlight, harder than he expected. "Stan prefers to read rather than avidly socialize. If you want to see a pair in which the two people have nothing in common, that's

Stan and me. Rod, however, is a great, amazing guy and a perfect boyfriend."

Liz crossed her arms tightly as Tim tried stretching his back out to ease the pain from the blow of the metal flashlight. That was the first time in a long time Liz had actually cursed. And she'd never cursed in front of Tim before.

They finally reached the edge of the forest. A small wooden shack appeared, surrounded by trees. It seemed to be falling apart; the windows had shattered, and the paint was chipping off, giving it a very grim appearance.

"What is that?" Liz shined her flashlight on the house.

"I think it's an old custodian shed. My parents told me that back in the fifties, custodians used to stay out here when they weren't working."

"That's horrifying."

"It's what poor scumbags do." Tim chuckled and slowly walked toward the house.

"Why are we out here, anyway?"

"You know exactly why. To investigate the shadow. I guess to add more mystery to the legend. Don't expect to find anything valuable, rich girl."

Liz scowled and touched the old door at the back of the shed. A protruding piece of wood jabbed her in the finger.

"Dammit!" Liz yelled behind gritted teeth.

Tim ran over to her. "What's wrong?"

"Do you have a bandage anywhere?"

"I don't carry bandages on me."

Liz quickly reached for her hip but remembered her handbag was inside her car. She sighed.

Then the door creaked open. The smell of mildew filled the air.

"Did you open that to scare me? Nice." Liz rolled her eyes, squeezing her thumb against her bleeding finger.

"No, I didn't," Tim answered.

"You're such a bad liar." Liz shook her head.

"Sure thing, rich girl." Tim opened the door farther, using his foot, and walked in.

With the help of the flashlight, the two found the inside of the old shack to be extensively dusty. Pieces of broken wood were strewn everywhere, and a smashed-in-half table sat in the middle of the room. A very old Dunkin' Donuts box filled with spider webs sat on the left section of the table.

"Hello?" Liz asked as she sat down on an old creaky sofa. "Hello?"

"Hello," a quiet, polite male voice responded.

"Tim? Seriously, stop trying to scare me. You're as funny as a cry for help." Liz shined the flashlight in Tim's eyes.

"I'm seriously not!" Tim shielded himself with his arms. His tinted glasses helped lessen the aggravating brightness. "Stop saying that!"

"Hello. How are you?" The voice changed its tone to one more ominous.

"Wait, who—" Tim put his hands on Liz's shoulders and shook them. "We should get going now."

"But my legs hurt so badly from all this walking. Besides, you're just trying to be creepy."

Liz suddenly realized that may have been a stupid response. They'd been walking for barely ten minutes and her legs hurt? She was thankful none of the others had heard her say something like that. Before Tim could respond to her, someone else spoke up.

"Let me massage them for you," the voice said.

"Who are you?" Liz asked, fear filling her voice.

"Don't ask; let's just get the hell out of here." Tim grabbed Liz's hand as they ran out of the shed.

The two bolted for Liz's house far in the distance. They ran straight ahead, hoping they'd taken the correct route. They heard running and breathing. Liz had no clue if the noises were their own or if they were being chased.

As if by luck, Tim and Liz found themselves out of the forest more quickly than they'd expected. They sprinted toward Liz's driveway and jumped into her white 1980 Corvette 305 parked in the driveway.

"Start the car!" Liz screamed as she handed him the keys from her handbag.

"Got it." Tim slammed on the pedal, and the car sped off down the road to the school.

Liz turned around and saw a figure waving slowly at them, a knife in his hands. "Is this thing watching us? What the hell is that?" She spun forward, brushing her brown hair back.

"I have no clue. I'm not looking back." Tim's words nearly stuck in his throat. He remained focused on the road with his hands clenching the wheel, his knuckles pale.

"Neither do I." Liz turned back around.

Neither spoke another word for the remainder of the drive.

Tim parked the car in the student lot before he and Liz ran to the front of the school. Their friends were waiting just outside, along with around thirty other classmates.

"What took you guys so long?" Veronica wrapped her arms around Tim's neck as they hugged firmly.

"There is a fucking killer in that fucking forest." Liz ran toward Richie and Rod, who caught her when she jumped on him. The guys, like Tim, were surprised Liz was actually cursing. Though Rod wasn't—she cursed when they were alone.

Thinking more about the man in the woods, Liz held Rod even tighter. Little things frightened her, from snakes to rats, so something like a mysterious man lurking in the woods by her house was gut-wrenching. As Rod wrapped an arm around her waist, Liz noticed Alan held the box of articles from her house in his hands.

"Steve left to pick up Tammy," Richie said.

"I'm scared!" Liz buried her face in Rod's chest. "My finger is bleeding, and there is a killer in that old custodian shed!"

"You mean the one behind the school?" Rod cocked an eyebrow while inspecting Liz's finger. It'd stopped bleeding by this point.

"Yes!" Liz whimpered.

"Calm down!" Veronica told Liz as students again began to focus on the group.

"We can't stay here tonight, and I'm starting to have doubts about going to the lake house, too, with all these strange occurrences. Two in one night is more than enough for me," Tim said.

"Two?" Rod asked.

Liz grabbed Rod's waist tightly, not wanting to let go of him. She knew she looked cowardly, but she didn't care. She brushed some of her hair away from her face. "We think we heard and saw someone out there."

"Please. Is Timmy scared?" Richie teased as he nudged Tim's shoulder.

"You didn't see what was out there, though." Tim pushed Richie away, keeping his voice calm. "That mess was creepy as hell. I wouldn't be surprised if you acted the same way."

"Timmy, please don't cry," Alan jeered as he and Rod laughed.

Tim breathed in heavily at his friend's comments, but Veronica held his hand to keep him from getting more wound up.

"Seriously! It was scary!" Liz whined.

"OK, kids, you can come in." The teacher unlocked the school doors and led them to the library.

The library in Franklin Pierce High School was enormous, sporting a vast wealth of books. It was neatly filled with wooden desks and lounge chairs all spread around. The walls were gray and the carpet dark blue.

While the thirty other kids lounged about in the middle, where a statue of fourteenth president Franklin Pierce stood, the group of friends moved on to the back of the library by one of the bookshelves.

"It's too bad we probably won't be able to do anything fun here except stay put and read articles," Alan said, leaning against the shelf.

"Agreed," Richie said as he flopped on the ground by Alan's feet.

Everyone else took his or her seat on the carpet. Alan slumped down and placed the box of articles in the middle of the group.

"That doesn't sound too bad you guys. I mean it could be worse, we could still be stuck outside," Veronica said looking at Liz and Tim. "Besides, be happy we're here now, Alan. Anyone who arrives later might find us all asleep.

"Sucks for them," Alan said. "Anyway, I say we break up and go find out more about Ray Kuiper."

"No!" Liz screamed.

"Yes!" Alan yelled back.

"Guys, c'mon. She's obviously scared. Leave her alone," Tim cut in.

The rest of the group stared in disbelief at Tim. Everyone knew Tim couldn't stand her, but all of a sudden, he was standing up for her? Maybe he was just agreeing with her because fear had clouded his judgment. Liz was shocked he was actually sticking up for her, but it made her feel appreciated, more than anything.

"You're only saying that because you're scared too, Timmy." Rod rolled his eyes. "Richie and Alan, go out to the custodian house. Veronica and I can go to the boiler room, and, Tim, you and Liz can stay here and read articles. Not too scary?"

"Fine," Liz said. "But I'm not going outside this library."

"That's why you're in here, babe." Rod stood up and kissed Liz on the cheek before he and Veronica walked out.

"Peace." Richie and Alan left too.

Liz found herself alone with Tim again. She glanced over at him. He was nearly slouching, completely silent. She looked back at the dried blood on her finger and thumb.

A couple of girls from the group of kids hanging out near the statue called Tim's name and waved. Tim smiled slightly and gestured back to them. But his eyes fell back on Liz, who was now primping with the help of a flip mirror, making sure her makeup hadn't gotten ruined from running outside.

"Let's get reading," Tim offered.

"Sounds good to me." Liz put her mirror away and pulled the old box of articles toward them.

Liz grabbed some articles and scooted against the bookcase to read. The moment she began to go over an article titled "Mysterious Circumstances regarding Death of Student," the doors opened, and in came Steve with Tammy Heston. Their hands intertwined as they spotted Liz and Tim in the back of the library and made their way over.

Steve wore an orange shirt and black pajama bottoms with boat shoes, while Tammy had on a Victoria's Secret lace pajama set.

Tim chuckled. "Tammy and my mother have the same taste."

A few inches shorter than Steve, Tammy had perfectly straight light-brown hair that went down to her chest, big brown eyes, and a seductive smile. Topping it all off was her tan skin—the product of sunbathing on her rooftop patio. Tammy also played on the school softball team, and she sported a mild bruise on her thigh from a game last week.

"Tammy, nice to see you." Tim invited Tammy and Steve to sit down next to him.

"Same to you, Tim," she replied. "Sharlene says hi."

"Bullshit, Tammy," Tim said calmly.

Liz nearly gasped. She'd heard this story before. Sharlene was one of Tammy's friends, but Liz had never met her. Back in freshman year, Tim apparently had had a small crush on her, but she completely shot him down. Well, she'd simply used him to do things for her. Tim now couldn't stand her, and Tammy was one of the girls who'd laughed in his face when he'd tried to ask Sharlene out.

"Elizabeth Carlough." Tammy focused on Liz and grinned, revealing a mild gap between her upper front teeth. "It's great to see you're here."

Liz rolled her eyes and groaned. The one girl she truly disliked. All because they'd worn the same dress during the winter formal three months ago. It seemed rather petty to hate Tammy over a dress, but when the dress happened to be a Halston, it was a completely different story.

"Tammy, cut the bullshit. Just leave me alone." Liz moved away from Tammy to sit next to Tim, on the other side of Steve.

"You're just jealous that Clarissa and Lauren didn't want you to hang out with them anymore," Tammy snapped back.

"Go die!" Liz screamed. The other students looked over toward them.

"Tammy, please." Tim looked at Tammy. "Cool off, and leave Liz alone."

"Hey!" Steve laughed. "Please, please, please. Now can't we all just get along?"

"No!" Liz whined as she buried her face in Tim's chest.

Steve stared at Tim and then at Liz. They were all reading one another's facial expressions. Liz could tell Steve thought something was going on between her and Tim. The fact the two guys had been best friends since kindergarten meant they knew each other well. Liz shook her head and parted her lips as Tammy broke the silence.

"Anyway, what are you guys doing?" Tammy asked.

"Looking at old articles," Tim responded. "About Ray Kuiper."

"Ray Kuiper?" Tammy laughed, cutting Tim off.

"For the love of God," Liz sneered. "Why is everything a joke with you?"

Tammy hesitated slightly and then continued. "Easy—because you yourself are a joke, and that's why I make them. I mean, other than you, who else hangs out with ugly people and dates hoods?"

"Get real, Tammy," Tim said.

Liz smiled at Tim. His new attitude toward her meant a lot. Tim smiled back in return.

"OK...you guys are acting freaky," Steve said. "Don't make me tell Rod," he warned.

"Tell Rod what?" Tim asked, looking as though he'd just heard the stupidest joke in the world. "C'mon, you know I love Veronica. I would never, ever, cheat on her."

"Rod is my life," Liz said blankly. "You're just jealous that Tim and I can find someone to be with while you're stuck with this slut." Liz pointed to Tammy, who clenched her teeth.

"That's it. Steve, let's go," Tammy hissed.

Tammy stood up and grabbed Steve's arms, yanking him up and dragging him out of the library with her. This left Liz and Tim alone once again.

"We should get back to work." Tim began to read the article on his lap. Liz grabbed a yearbook and flipped through the pages.

"Wait a minute. Here's a group picture of some students from your class from last year's yearbook. Isn't that Ray Kuiper?" Liz pointed at the picture.

"Liz, that's impossible." Tim glanced at the picture. "Your eyes must be playing tricks on you. That's Alan."

"Oh. They look alike."

"They really do. But find nineteen fifty-two. You won't find anything in our junior yearbook."

Liz quickly found a red-and-gold-striped yearbook from the shelf behind her and blew dust off it. She coughed lightly and opened it. "I'll have to find something in here, right?"

"It'd be strange if you didn't."

Moments of silence passed between Tim and Liz. The only noise they could hear was the sound of the other teenagers playing truth or dare. A couple of the students asked Tim and Liz to come over and play the game with them, but the two declined. The old mementos were far more interesting than daring someone to lick the carpet, or whatever ridiculous stunt their classmates could come up with.

"I'm sorry to abruptly change the subject, Liz, but I'm wondering, why do you *really* hate Tammy?" Tim chuckled slightly.

Liz's eagerness turned dull. The last topic she wished to talk about was Tammy, but she felt Tim had the right to know. It was bizarre, but in the events of the past couple of hours, she sensed a closer bond to Tim. They went from mutual disdain—though that was stronger on his part—to talking like they were close friends all of a sudden. But Liz loved it. She felt welcome, like the group was no longer a completely hostile environment.

"Because she's loose. She slept with practically every guy I tried going out with, except Rod...and Stan, of course. Clarissa and Lauren are idiots. Tammy slept with their boyfriends, and yet they still hang with her. But when they found out I went on one date with Stan back in freshman year, not to mention how Tammy and I had the same dress for winter formal, they got rid of me like I was garbage. I can't believe Steve would even go out with Tammy. She's a nymphomaniac, anyway."

"Well, I've known Steve for a long time. That's basically what he loves. You know—a sex lover, huh?" Tim and Liz smiled at each other, trying to contain their laughter.

Liz couldn't believe she was actually having a conversation with Tim that didn't involve trading barbs that left her pouting and upset. Slowly he was becoming a friend she never knew she'd have.

"Yeah." Liz couldn't keep it in anymore and began laughing.

"I wonder what they're doing now," Tim said nonchalantly.

"You know what they're doing," Liz teased.

"Eh, maybe. But why think about it?"

As fun as this was for Liz, the story and mystery of Ray Kuiper made for a much more interesting conversation, even if the whole ordeal frightened her beyond belief. "Keep reading!" Liz urged.

"I hate Tammy too," Tim said out of the blue.

Then it was silent as they shared another brief moment of stares from each other. Who knew that two people who had barely tolerated each other in the morning could end up revealing new facts about themselves by night?

"Never heard that before," Liz whispered as she looked away.

"It's true." Tim shrugged. "I prefer you over her. You're not as annoying as people see you to be."

"Worse." She forced a smile on her face. "Correction: I am worse."

"Touché."

"Keep reading!"

Tim grinned as he scanned the article he held in his hand. Suddenly he grabbed Liz's hand. "I found something! Check this out." He pointed to an old article titled "Missing Teenager Spotted."

"It says Ray Kuiper was spotted in this school and around Charleston in the late fifties, sixties, and seventies," he said.

"That leaves the late eighties. Good thing we'll be graduated."

"You can say that again," Tim agreed. "It also says the sightings occurred around the winter formal, which has already passed. They are said to be 'strange.' Friends of Kuiper say that he never had a date to the winter formal and was going to ask Susan Finn." Tim's smile dropped. "That's Veronica's mother."

"You're joking." Liz's mouth gaped.

"It says he planned to ask her but that she ended up going with Robert Leeds—Veronica's father—before he ever got the chance."

"This is crazy," Liz stated in disbelief. "You don't think Mrs. Leeds was the reason he died or disappeared?"

"I think that maybe it had to do with girls. Mr. Leeds had a motive."

"Keep reading!" Liz urged.

Tim quickly scanned the rest of the article. "It says that December fifteenth was the last day he was seen." He frowned.

"Is that it?"

"Yep." Tim tossed the article back in the box.

A couple of the girls in the truth-or-dare group came over and again asked the two if they wanted to play. Tim shook his head.

"We should go check on Veronica," Tim said.

"You can go. I'll stay here. The last thing I want to do is leave this practical sanctuary."

Tim laughed. "Why don't you go join the group playing?"

"I guess. Why not?"

Liz rose up and bent forward to stretch her legs before joining the other students in the center of the library. She watched as Tim took a few deep breaths and walked out of the room.

The halls were dim, and all the posters seemed to jump out at him. He wasn't scared, but he was shaking. He began taking quiet, slow steps down the hallway. He debated on going back to the shed in the woods or the storage room. Alan and Richie weren't exactly the most sensible guys. If there *was* a killer lurking in the custodian house, would they make it? Tim spun around and ran out of the school through the bulky back doors. The cold air stung his skin as he ran to the forest. Tears developed in his eyes, as if he was running to his death. Fear overtook him. All sorts of memories, from his earliest—his third birthday—to his most recent milestones, flooded his thoughts, and he considered everything he would be giving up.

He just knew there was a killer in those woods with a knife. And he was sure that going back in there was the stupidest thing in the world. But if his time to go happened to be now, then so be it; otherwise, fate would find some way to keep him alive. He reached the shed.

The ground beneath him was wet and muddy. The door stood wide open, waiting for him to come in. Tim searched his surroundings. The perfect place to be murdered. No one would ever come back here, except maybe a few of his friends. Tim slowly stepped into the shed. Empty—just like he'd expected.

"I'm dead," he whispered. Suddenly a cold hand touched the back of his neck.

"Richie!" Alan yelled. "Oh, hey, Tim!"

Tim emitted a few sighs of relief as his palpitating heart slowed back to a steady beat.

"Sorry if I scared you, bro." Richie laughed. "This shack is disturbing for sure. But we found a few items that prove someone lives here."

"Give it to him," Alan said, tapping a flashlight against his thigh.

"The sofa is very warm. I doubt you and Liz were sitting on it long enough for you to heat it up like that." Richie raised an eyebrow. "There's food in the fridge—fresh food. And there's fresh blood and a knife in the bathroom."

Fresh blood and a knife? That was all Tim needed to hear as he moved toward the door. "We should get out of here," he urged.

"Oh, Timmy, calm down!" Alan laughed. "What are you worried about?"

"Let's go find Veronica," Tim said.

"She's fine," Richie insisted.

"I want to check on her!" Tim shouted.

All of a sudden, the door slammed shut and the lights switched on. Tim, Alan, and Richie jumped up and huddled together next to the sofa. If things weren't nerve-racking now, the three friends had no idea what was.

"Who's there?" Alan yelled.

"Why would you ask that? Are you expecting them to say, 'Over here'?" Tim forced a laughed.

"G-guys…" Richie stammered, pointing to the door.

And there it was. Tim had had a feeling they'd find something in the shed; he'd figured that out on the way here. He knew something about this story was more than just a legend, and he'd tried to pressure everyone into learning more about it. Now a torn, red-streaked sheet of paper hung before them, pinned to the door by a knife. But how long had it been there? When Tim had arrived, the door had been wide open, and he could see the front. Then it closed, and this note was there.

He read the penciled words aloud: "I can't wait to meet each and every one of you."

"What the fuck?" they all whispered.

"Who the hell wrote this!" Tim shouted at Alan.

"I don't know, but we need to leave," Alan replied, opening the door without touching the note or knife.

"That's the knife we found in the bathroom." Richie grabbed Tim's wrist as they ran deep into the dark.

Anything can happen in the darkness; unlike the daytime, you can't see what's coming at you. Nighttime is the perfect time for a killer to strike. Alan was thankful he had the flashlight as they ran through the forest toward the school.

They ran faster than they thought their legs could take them. Each one of them could hear the others breathe, assuring him that they were all still together. There was a killer in the forest—and a strong chance it was chasing them.

"What do you think that note meant?" Alan asked.

Tim felt his feet begin to sink in the wet soil.

"It's not time for stupid questions, Alan!" Richie yelled.

"It's too good to be true!" Alan stopped running and turned around.

"Where are you going?" Tim called. He and Richie stopped in their tracks and looked back. "Where are you going?" Tim yelled again.

"Back to get the note!" Alan said as he disappeared into the darkness. With the flashlight.

"Idiot," Richie whispered. "Should we wait?"

"I—I don't know."

"He's an idiot."

"I know."

"He's dead meat!"

"I know."

"We have to wait for him."

"I know," Tim whispered as he and Richie stood in silence.

4

KILLER

They were still waiting. They figured it was midnight, most likely. Tim and Richie had been waiting for ten minutes, and Alan still hadn't returned. Tim had spent the entire time listening to Richie's feet pace back and forth in the damp soil. They could've left at any time, but they wouldn't abandon Alan. They'd never do something like that, even if their lives depended on it.

"We are not going to leave Alan." Tim looked at Richie, who nodded in agreement.

The wind howled as they looked out into the distance toward where Alan had run off. The main question was whether Alan was still alive. The entire event proved hair-raising, from the sudden note to Alan racing back for it—and the possibility that a killer was stalking them in the forest.

"Alan is stupid," Richie said.

"I know" was all Tim could get out.

"Why would he try to get some stupid note? Is he out of his mind?"

"True…risking his life for something like that," Tim said, but Richie failed to hear him.

"Alan is damn stupid!" Richie screamed.

But all of a sudden, to the surprise of both guys, a voice called through the forest. They were frightened at first, but when they recognized the voice's familiar tone, their fears were put to rest.

"It's just me, guys!" Alan shouted.

Tim saw the beam of the flashlight approaching. Alan was holding on to the note in the same hand as his flashlight. He hadn't retrieved the knife that had once pinned it to the door of the shed.

"I don't even know why you wanted to go back and get it," Richie remarked.

Tim found himself smiling in relief, only because Alan had come back safely. Seeing someone risk his or her life does strange things to a person. Death could stimulate sympathy from anyone unless he was heartless.

"Alan," Tim whispered. "Aren't you gonna answer the question?"

"This note is proof," Alan responded, briefly looking at the note as he shined the flashlight on it. The hole in the paper was larger from Alan's tearing it from the knife. "Proof that someone lives in that shed. Either that or someone else is playing a stupid prank on us."

"It probably is a prank," Richie insisted. "Why don't we all go back there and confront this asshole?"

"Are you crazy? What if it's not? Then what are we gonna do when we find a killer inside the shed?" Tim whispered words he wanted to shout.

"No way am I going back there." Alan placed the paper into the pocket of his pajama bottoms and held up his hands—wearing black gloves. They were his driving gloves, which he had retrieved from his locker before heading out with Richie, just in case. "I'm *not* stupid."

"Yes you are." Richie put his arms around Alan and Tim as they began walking again.

None of them were going back to the shed. The knife and the note with the red streaks all over it were enough to steer them away from it as much as possible. The incident in the woods was the first time in a very long time that the three teenagers had been freaked out by a sight like this. Tim only wanted to get back inside the school and never set foot in the shed again. Could it have been a prank? Possibly. But if it hadn't been, God knows what could've happened back there. Everyone picked up speed.

"The custodians should consider themselves lucky they don't go out there anymore," Tim said.

"No one should have to stay in that dump, except for some killer," Richie replied.

"But now we can go find Veronica." Alan nudged Tim in the stomach as they walked back to the school.

As relief struck Tim, he imagined the shed again. But this time he thought of the time he'd spent with Liz a few hours earlier. There just had to be someone inside that shed. The creepy male voice and those strange actions. He hadn't forgot the entire ordeal one bit.

Still, the likelihood of it being a prank was high. When he and Liz had heard the voice earlier, students were just beginning to arrive at the school for the sleepover. One of them could've snuck into the shed to joke around. But how could the person have known Tim and Liz would be going back there? And besides, no one else ever went back there for any reason.

"Are you sure it could've been a prank, Alan?" Tim said after some silence.

"Does a bear shit in the woods?" Alan forced a laugh.

"It just doesn't seem likely."

"That someone decided to prank us?"

"Bullshit," Richie said to Tim.

"I'm serious," Tim continued.

They walked in silence until they opened the doors to the back of the school, having moved through the courtyard. A haunting, chilling sensation rushed through Tim's body, and he found himself thinking about running around the school to find Steve. A world without his best friend, Steve—he couldn't even imagine it. College next year without him would be like a world without Veronica. He didn't think he could survive.

Tim paused by the door to the theater. A soft moaning was coming from inside. He didn't want to imagine the things that could be happening—or who they could be happening to. *Veronica! If anyone is hurting Veronica, I will…*Tim took a deep breath as he held the handle to open the door, ripping the flashlight from Alan's hand. *Veronica! Oh my gosh.*

"Let go of her!" Tim yelled as he drew open the doors.

Silence followed. Darkness was once again all he could see. Then the moaning started again, followed by heavy breathing and ending with a deep groan. Tim began searching around the theater, tracking the sound. He was running into chairs, but Tim knew damn well the pain of losing his friends would hurt more than the bruises he would receive from this.

Finally he stopped by the prop room—the source of the moans. Tim shined the flashlight on the door. A bloody handprint was smeared on it. *This is it, Tim.* Flashbacks of the figure in the shed came to him once more. He tried to view his future, but death was the only thing he saw.

"Tim!" He heard Alan's voice from behind him.

"You OK, man?" Richie's soft mumbling voice followed after.

"Over here, guys," Tim managed to say. "I heard moaning...I can't...If this is Veronica..." He was trying to hold back tears but let one flow. Thankfully Richie and Alan couldn't see it in the dark.

"C'mon—it's just a stupid prank. Obviously one of the other students staying here is bullshitting us." Richie daringly opened the prop-room door.

Tim, Alan, and Richie stood in the doorway, unable to see a thing. Worse and worse visions of Veronica being dead flooded Tim's mind. This wasn't the end; this was crueler. The moaning continued even after he opened the door. The doors were heavy and made no sound. In the darkness, the three guys could see nothing that indicated anything bad.

"Tim, you flick the light switch on when I tell you," Alan whispered almost inaudibly. "Richie, come with me."

"Got it," Tim agreed.

Alan and Richie carefully walked through the blackness and closer to the moans. Tim stood by the door, his hand running along the wall to find the light switch. He felt it and readied for the cue.

"Now!" Alan shouted.

Tim flipped the switch on and heard a scream. He ran past a rack of hanging dresses and suits, where he found a sight that caused him to stop right where he was. Steve was on a lime-green couch lying on top of her—Tammy. The two of them froze entirely, as did the guys. Tammy turned three shades of red. Steve did too.

"Guys, what the fuck?" Tammy yelled as she pushed Steve off her, covering herself up with one of the prop dresses. Steve ended up falling off the couch and quickly threw his pajama bottoms over his waist. He was frowning irritably at his friends.

"Oh shit." Richie looked down, trying so hard not to laugh that tears formed in his eyes. "We are so sorry, man," he said, embarrassment filling his voice as he turned away quickly.

"Dude, Tammy." Alan raised his eyebrows. "I mean, now that we're here and you're here, I guess—Tammy, you've got a nice rack."

"Come on, Alan!" Steve shouted, astounded.

"W-we heard moaning coming from here, and we thought someone may have been…dying," Tim said.

Tammy's right eye twitched. She looked mortified by the fact that people had walked in on her and Steve having sex, but add the fact that they wouldn't leave—that they even had the gall to try to engage in conversation while a skimpy dress just barely covered her nude body—and maybe her growing anger was understandable.

"Well, obviously you're wrong!" Tammy yelled again. "Now get the hell out!"

"Yeah…" Steve said to the guys. Then he slyly smiled as he glanced up at Tammy from the carpet, his eyes reading suggestively.

"You too!" She hit him on the back of the head, and he stumbled up, grabbing his boxers and throwing them on as the four guys quickly made their way to the door.

They could all hear Tammy sighing furiously as Steve caught up with Alan, Richie, and Tim, fully clothed but with sweat all over his body. He was more than distressed by the actions of his pals, even though it had been accidental.

"You gonna be all right in here?" Steve called out to her.

"I need some time to cool off," Tammy shot back from behind the clothes rack.

"Well, if you need any help getting dressed, I—" Steve began.

"Would you all get out?" Tammy fumed.

As they left the room, Tim noticed that the blood he thought had been smeared on the door appeared to be just paint. He investigated more closely, and he saw it was chipping. Now all Tim knew was that he wanted to find Veronica right away.

"That was awkward," Richie said, grinning nervously.

"You don't say," Steve scowled. He pushed the bill of Alan's baseball cap down over his eyes. "Haven't you clowns ever heard of knocking, for Pete's sake?"

"It's not like we meant to barge in, man," Richie said, attempting to save face.

The four found their way out of the theater and back into the library. Liz and Rod were cuddling near the articles. She giggled as he kissed her chin a couple of times. And Veronica had her arm resting on one of the smaller bookshelves, waiting for the others to return. Tim let out a big sigh of relief. He ran over and hugged her with all his might. Alan, Richie, and Steve stood together by the librarian's desk.

"Hey, guys." Rod let go of Liz and stood up.

"Rod, man, did you find anything in the boiler room?" Alan asked.

"No. Not one little thing." Rod sighed.

"It's true. We looked all over the place and found nothing," Veronica added.

"Any luck with you guys?" Liz asked Tim.

Tim gave Liz a simple shake of the head.

"Although"—Richie smirked as he eyed Steve—"we did catch Steve scoring with Tammy."

Rod, Veronica, and Liz snickered at the revelation, much to Steve's dismay. He threatened to hit Richie for disclosing those details.

"Oh wow," Veronica remarked between giggles. "How did that look?"

"Picture this: Steve getting hit upside the head by Tammy, and before that, he fell off the couch in the prop room." Tim smiled.

As the laughter grew louder, Steve's face turned red. Steve didn't get embarrassed easily—he could manage well without risking humiliation—but this was one of the rare occasions it happened, and Steve wished he could disappear right then and there.

"Anyway." Rod stopped laughing, and seriousness overtook him. "I almost forgot to tell the rest of you. I know this may sound crazy, but Veronica and I thought we heard a scream while we were in the boiler room."

"What? When did this happen?" Richie asked.

"Right when we entered," Veronica said.

"You don't say," Tim wondered aloud.

"Why didn't you say that earlier, Rod?" Liz chimed in.

"I don't know."

It wasn't like the events that had taken place out in the forest were just going to disappear. The note could never leave the thoughts of the three boys who'd searched the shed minutes earlier. And Alan had it in his pocket. He fished it out and reread it silently.

"Well...we did find this in the woods. We didn't hear a scream, but we think this is one big prank," Richie whispered to make sure the other students, who were all lying on the carpet in a circle talking among themselves, didn't overhear the group.

Rod, Veronica, and Liz said nothing. Surely the boys should've mentioned that sooner. The three of them analyzed the note.

"Why didn't you tell us?" Veronica asked.

Before anyone could answer, Rod rushed to the door and ran out, causing a few of the other kids to watch him in surprise. It was sudden and strange for Rod to react like that. What the hell was he going to do? Was the talk of strange happenings making him sick?

"What! No, there's a real killer out there," Liz whispered harshly.

"Creepy stuff did happen out there, but I think we're just being pranked. That scream was a prank; this note is a freaking prank too. Some asshole wants his ass beat—that's why he's doing this." Richie rolled his eyes. "It's just a fucking legend. Everything we read at Liz's house is just a fucking legend."

"Just a legend?" Veronica cocked an eyebrow. "You find a note covered in what looks like dried blood, and we hear a scream that makes all the hairs on my arm stand up. And now you tell me the one piece of information we have that might explain them is just a fucking legend?" she yelled.

The other kids in the library now had their eyes on the group, stunned at Veronica's sudden outburst. But this time the group didn't care; right now, only the shed mattered.

"Let's go, guys." Tim put his arm around Veronica.

"And if we all don't come out alive?" Liz whimpered.

"May the best of us survive." Steve laughed.

"And I will prove to you guys that it's just a legend." Richie sarcastically smiled. "If this whole ordeal isn't a prank, then, well, dumb-ass me."

And with that, they all ran out of the library, chasing after Rod and ignoring the others, who were calling them to come back.

5

FACT OR FICTION

"It's one ten. We have, like, ten million more hours to go," Liz whined. They had caught up to Rod in the student parking lot, which was illuminated by streetlights. Everyone kept a close eye on him so he wouldn't run off alone.

"But today we get to go to the lake house." Alan tapped the flashlight against his thigh.

"I still can't believe your parents said yes," Richie said, patting Alan's back.

"Well, my father and I have a close bond." Alan began talking in a Shakespearean accent. "But 'twas my mother who I had to get the majority of trust from."

"Well, Lorraine and Albert are killing me." Tim frowned. "Mom's been nagging me more than usual."

"Sounds like Tammy," Richie remarked, nudging Steve's shoulder.

All the guys laughed as Steve high-fived Richie. Veronica shook her head, but Liz shoved Richie. He kept his wise-guy grin, though. He didn't mean it in a rude or even misogynistic way. By this point, conflict was common between Richie and Liz. Every time he tried acting like himself with the guys, Liz always gave him glances or shoved him. While they might have gotten along occasionally, she still pissed him off almost every day.

"You boys are so simpleminded," Veronica jokingly said. "Do you guys talk about anything other than sex, money, and booze?"

The boys exchanged silent glances.

"No," Steve nonchalantly replied.

"Not really!" Alan exclaimed.

"But I love you." Tim leaned in and kissed Veronica on the cheek.

"Yeah, yeah, yeah." Liz rolled her eyes and pushed through Richie and Steve to get to her boyfriend. "Rod, I don't want you going out there. Look—I prepared a list of all the guys in the group I am fine with dying." Liz said, pulling a folded-up piece of paper from her handbag. "Here goes…"

Richie thought this was unbelievable. *Are you fucking kidding me, Liz?* he thought. Fine with dying? Was this a joke? Then again, was Liz saying it? Yes. Was it a joke? Had to be. Richie and the other guys, excluding Rod, gave Liz the most inane-looking grins known to man.

"This should be good," Richie whispered to Tim, smirking.

"Richie," Liz said calmly.

"Of course!" he shouted. "What the hell, Liz?"

"Alan."

"I was so expecting Steve," Alan whispered to Tim.

"And Steve," Liz said, finishing the list and placing back in her handbag.

"What about Tim?" Richie asked, waving his arms dramatically.

Steve glanced at Tim, making a skeptical face. Tim cocked an eyebrow. He opened his mouth, ready to speak, before Steve spoke up and cut him off swiftly.

"It wouldn't surprise me," Steve said and then took a deep breath.

"What was that supposed to mean?" Tim hit Steve hard in the shoulder. Steve grabbed the shoulder firmly.

"You're overreacting." Veronica laughed, patting Steve on the shoulder Tim had just struck. "And it looks like you, Alan, and Richie are going out." She pointed to the woods, which were shrouded in darkness.

"I have a feeling the killer is still there," Alan said.

"I don't think I want Steve out there," Tim said nervously. "I don't know what I would do if he died."

"Aw, Timmy, save that speech for the wedding." Richie laughed.

Tim scowled and raised his middle finger at Richie. It wasn't uncommon for Richie to make jokes at Tim's expense; he'd been doing that for nearly four years now.

"I didn't hear about a wedding." Steve teasingly put his arm around Tim and laughed.

Alan was the first person to walk off, but everyone followed after him. Despite Liz's bringing up the possibility of death, the friends ventured out into the darkness of the woods.

It took some time to get back to the shed, but with the help of Alan's flashlight, the group made it. Alan stopped everyone before he shined the flashlight directly at the shed. Richie took a deep breath. Just because he'd already been inside the old custodian shack didn't mean he was prepared to go back inside again, prank or not.

The group could hear the leaves rustling on trees limbs above. Insects chirped and buzzed somewhere deep in the darkness. Richie waited for one of their classmates to turn the lights on and jump out in front of them. He clenched a fist, ready to deck in the face anyone who dared to do so.

"So, this is where we found the note." Alan breathed in deeply. "I suppose you just have to see the inside of the shed for yourselves."

Bravely Alan opened the door to the shed and walked inside. The lights were off, so he flicked the switch. The inside of the shed looked almost exactly the same as before. Except this time there was writing on the wall. Veronica stepped back, stunned by the sight. Liz almost screamed as she grabbed Rod's arm and clung to him. Rod held his girlfriend close to him, but his reaction didn't change. The words "Nothing will remain the same" had been carved deep into the plaster.

"That wasn't there before," Tim said on behalf of Richie and Alan.

"But it's just as stupid." Richie rolled his eyes.

Richie stepped up to the wall and ran his finger over the carving. *Made with the knife, of course,* he thought. He smiled, containing his laughter. The whole scenario seemed to be growing into a bigger farce. Nobody appeared unexpectedly, and nobody made a noise; Richie figured that whoever was doing this was probably cracking up behind the old custodian house.

"Liz, why the hell do you look like you're having a heart attack?" Steve asked. "If anything, this is only making me agree more with Richie."

"Thank you!" Richie grinned.

One by one, everyone left the custodian house. It was official: this entire situation was stupid. Richie began to chuckle as Alan turned the lights off. Soon, everyone but Liz began to laugh. They'd been pranked, and it was all in good taste, if sort of creepy. It had worked.

"Where to now?" Veronica asked casually.

"Back inside the school, I guess." Alan pointed his flashlight on the grass. "Time to go join the others and hang out. Though part of me wants to go home now, honestly."

"Why not go back to one of our houses and spend the night?" Steve offered. "If anything, I'm looking more forward to the lake house than this sleepover. Had you fuckers not screwed me over," Steve said, shooting a dirty look at Richie, Alan, and Tim, "I'd still be with Tammy."

"Let's go back to my house, then," Liz suggested. "It's big enough for all of us."

"Fine with me," Veronica replied. She grabbed Tim's hand, and the two began making their way out of the woods. Everyone followed suit.

In all honesty, Richie wanted to find this prankster. He, or she, could be lurking by the entrance to the woods, by the parking lot. Of course, if it were a female prankster, Richie wouldn't mind. He'd end up asking for her number. A guy prankster, on the other hand, would get a fist directly to his face for trying to be funny.

"Won't your parents mind us being at your place, Liz?" Alan asked. "Especially since this is last second."

"Maybe," Liz said to Alan while locking eyes with Rod. "But it's not like they'll kick you all out or anything."

"Not even your dad?" Rod said.

"I promise he won't do anything."

The group of teenagers finally made it from the woods into the brightly lit parking lot. Richie was a bit disappointed that no one jumped out to scare them, but so be it. He went directly to his car, Alan in tow. Steve was going back into the school to say good-bye to Tammy, while Tim and Veronica were going in her car. Liz was bringing Rod back to her house.

"That was fun, wasn't it, Rich?" Alan chuckled.

"Oh yeah, a bunch of running around in the dark forest thinking there's a killer stalking the premises. And behind our school, to wrap it all up!" Richie smirked. He unlocked his burgundy 1973 Ford Mustang and sat in the driver's seat. Alan rode shotgun and took off his baseball cap.

"Makes you a bit unsure about fact or fiction, though, doesn't it?"

"Maybe a little bit," Richie admitted. "Do you still have that note?"

"Yeah." Alan fished the note out of his pajama pocket and handed it to Richie.

Richie went over the note—"I can't wait to meet each and every one of you"—a couple of times and then snickered and tossed it onto the backseat. Words written in pencil and red streaks that looked more like watercolor than blood. A stroke of *genius* there.

"Time to head to Liz's," Alan groaned.

"Fun, fun," Richie said, mimicking Liz, as he drove out of the student parking lot.

At Liz's house, most of the teenagers sat together on the couch, with Alan and Steve sitting on lounge chairs. They were sitting silently, watching a rerun of *The Tomorrow Show* with Tom Snyder on NBC. To the teenagers, Tom was hip. His interview of KISS was what had turned them on to the show.

"Sweetheart, why are you back so early?" Liz's mother's voice stunned Richie. He had forgotten that it was high and annoying, just like Liz's.

Beverly Carlough looked like an older version of Liz, except her hair was a golden color and styled in a shoulder-length bob, thinned out at the ends and flipped up. Despite her voice, though, Richie and the others found Mrs. Carlough very friendly and sociable. She was very laid-back, the complete opposite of her husband. She was also a damn good real-estate agent—the leading Realtor in Charleston.

"We got bored, Mom." Liz rolled her eyes and rested an arm on Rod's shoulder. Rod kissed her forehead. He awkwardly exchanged glances with Richie, who grinned in a silly manner.

Richie had first met Rod in sixth grade, and they got along pleasantly, for the most part. But even after knowing each other for about six years, they wouldn't call each other best friends. Even "good friends" was a bit of a stretch. All along, Richie wondered what Rod saw in Liz. Annoying, clingy, dependent Liz.

"Oh. Well, I'll make you all strudels with hot chocolate. How does that sound?" Mrs. Carlough smiled.

"Perfect." Veronica nodded in approval. Liz's mother strolled out peacefully.

Then it was dead silent among the group, with only the television providing any sound.

Richie didn't know whether to start the conversation—or what he would say if he did. What was appropriate to talk about, and how would he say it? Until Liz's mother spoke up, no one had said a word since they'd arrived at the house. What was there to talk about right now? The upcoming fun at the lake house? The prank at the school?

Or had it been a prank? Richie hated the scenario entirely. As much as he wanted to stop thinking about it, it slipped back into his thoughts again. And what about that "bloody" handprint on the door where they'd found Steve? Richie had glanced at it for a second as he left the prop room with Tim and Alan, but he seemed to have forgotten about it until now. Could it have been dried blood? And even if it was paint, why was it there?

Richie guessed everyone had forgotten about all of that. He didn't blame them. So much happened afterward that it didn't matter anymore. He only felt sympathy for the people stuck in the school still… even Tammy. He figured that if there was a killer, those people could possibly be in danger, and yet here he and his friends were, safe in Liz's house. *No one should ever be in that type of scenario. Then again, it would be funny if Tammy got frightened, at the very least.* He never liked her from the moment he met her in middle school. Elitists could go to hell, for all he cared. Richie smiled at his thought.

"What are you smiling for, bucko?" Steve raised an eyebrow.

"Just had a funny thought—that's it," Richie said.

"Like what?" Liz popped her head up.

Richie paused but kept the smile intact. He knew Steve would hit him if he admitted he was thinking about Tammy getting spooked by the killer—or whoever this person was. Trying to focus only on his friends, Richie kept playing along.

"Nothing," Richie continued.

"C'mon—tell us," Alan badgered.

"It had to have been funny for you to smile about it, Richie," Tim said.

"Yeah, well…you all are just trying to distance yourselves from reality by distracting yourselves," Veronica said quietly, not bothering to be discreet. "I say we talk about it—the note."

"You want to discuss the prank, Veronica?" Rod asked, wrapping an arm around Liz. "Why? What point is there to that?"

"It just seems weird the prankster didn't pop out and say 'fooled you' or something," Veronica said.

"Look." Richie sat up from the couch. If this was to be the topic, he wanted to see how far he could take it. "If Ray Kuiper is on the loose, we should get out of town."

"How do we know this creeper is Ray Kuiper?" Liz asked.

"We don't; we're only assuming. I must admit it's a bit of a coincidence—learning about Ray Kuiper and then we're the ones who discover a note and the carving in the woods right after," Richie stated. He smiled at Alan, who was grinning back at him. The two of them sometimes grinned at each other for no apparent reason. It was just out of fun.

"Coincidence? Listen, go get a room queers," Steve joked as he cleared his throat, "this is too funny. Richie, you thought it was a prank, though. Are you seriously trying to say you now think other-wise? Listen here." He stood up as if to take a stance. "We're seniors; we cannot be held back by thinking about Ray Kuiper or a dumb-ass prank."

"That was the stupidest thing you have said all night, Steve." Veronica laughed.

Steve frowned and flopped back on the lounge chair he'd been sitting on.

"Actually..." Richie started. "Never mind."

"Oh, c'mon, Richie!" Alan said. "Tell us."

"Tammy." Richie finally offered. "We use Tammy as bait to see who this real killer is. If she dies"—Richie saw Steve glaring at him—"or we save her before she gets killed, we then go to the police. Good?"

"Good," everyone but Steve said in unison.

"No!" Steve yelled.

Liz's mom came back in and gave each of them a strudel and hot chocolate, and then she left.

"I'm not gonna let you guys kill Tammy," Steve continued. "I'm falling in love with her, for Christ's sake."

"You said the exact same words in regard to Brenda Ward and Lori Turner." Veronica rolled her eyes.

"Then there was Sandra Parker," Tim added.

"And Mary Reed." Alan laughed.

"Let's not forget your little crush on Dawn Martinez," Richie joked, and everyone else laughed.

The reference to Dawn Martinez caused Steve to hiccup. His head drooped at the mention of her name; she was his one true weakness.

"Dawn was more than a little crush. Hell, she was my longest-lasting girlfriend. Two years..." Steve gulped, sulking.

Richie could see in Steve's face that he still loved her. He and the others knew it too. Guiltily Richie couldn't believe he'd said that, and he realized it was a mistake. No one ever dared to bring up Dawn Martinez around Steve.

Why can't I just keep my damn mouth shut sometimes? Richie wondered.

"Besides," Steve said, hastily changing the subject, "Alan, what happened with you and Samantha Garfield? You two on-off status again?"

Alan groaned. "Yes, we are. I tell you—we have such strong feelings for each other, but we argue about the stupidest things, I swear."

Richie noticed Rod staring off, away from the others. He was physically there, but mentally he wasn't. Richie leaned over and shook Rod's shoulders lightly.

"What's happening, Rod?" Richie asked, bringing Rod out his fog.

"Huh? Oh, nothing, man." Rod let out a deep breath. "Maybe it's just...I still can't—and I'm about to bring it back up again—but I just can't stop thinking about those messages, regardless of whether it was a prank."

"Well, we can always go back and check the carving." Alan snickered.

Liz irritably pinched Alan's shoulder as a way to tell him off. He winced and quickly swiped her hand away.

"Alan, shut up," Liz stated.

"Rod, control your bossy princess." Richie took a quick glance at Liz. "Someone let the rich bitch out of her cage early."

"Bet it was Rod." Alan laughed, grabbing his throbbing arm.

"Now we know who her master is." Steve smiled, Dawn apparently no longer on his mind.

Rod slapped his forehead in frustration. Richie calling Liz a bitch was common by now. Rod had told Richie time and time again that he'd beat the hell out of Richie for saying that. But Richie persisted, and Rod had just come to the conclusion that Richie was kidding.

"Guys, c'mon," Tim cut in. "Leave Liz alone."

"Oh, Prince Timmy came to the rescue." Richie raised his voice to a high-pitched English accent. "Oh, Timmy. Timmy, save me!"

Tim closed his eyes to vent his anger at being called Timmy three times in one sitting. Alan's and Steve's laughing didn't help, nor did Veronica's small chuckle. Richie knew Tim hated the name. This was more of his antagonizing Tim.

"Guys, shut up!" Liz clenched her fists.

"Now Princess Liz is here to save her Prince Charming. Please. I know something is going on between you guys," Richie said in his normal voice.

"Nothing is going on." Liz looked at Rod, who acknowledged her.

"Ha, yeah," Veronica whispered. "Let's get back to business."

"This is business. Tim, are you and Liz..." Steve trailed off.

"No, no, no!" Tim and Liz shouted together.

"OK, then." Rod cleared his throat. "Like Veronica said, let's get back to business."

6

RUNNERS

Business, if there was any, didn't go anywhere near as planned. After laughing a little bit more, Richie and Alan had a side talk about girls, while Liz told Rod how happy she was about spending the ensuing week with him. Steve resumed watching the television as Veronica and Tim fixed silent stares at each other.

In that short nonverbal exchange, Tim read all her thoughts. *Are you cheating on me?* she asked him.

Never, he answered. A flashback aired in his mind. It was from sophomore year, when Tammy had pestered Tim to take her to the winter formal dance since Veronica was sick that weekend. Even though he didn't go, that flashback was powerful to Tim. Just like this moment was.

Honestly Veronica's questioning of him was a bit understandable. Since they'd begun dating, Veronica had something of a jealous quality emerge whenever other girls would talk to Tim longer than a couple of minutes. She would become impatient, and if Tim said something to a girl that came across as flirting, Veronica responded with a harsh glare. But nothing got her more worked up than when Tim shared smiles with other girls for long moments. Other than instances like those, Veronica was completely tranquil.

Are you cheating on me? her expression continued to ask. Tim didn't know what to say. He technically wasn't—and he was never going to—but that wasn't to say his thoughts about Liz were clean either.

Never. Tim shook his head, and Veronica smiled before turning to watch the television with Steve.

Tim felt his world spin as he zoned out. He didn't want Veronica to think that way. Tim didn't spend all of middle school falling head over heels in love with Veronica just to cheat on her and break her heart.

He trusted Steve was only kidding about the accusations. He'd given Liz one smile, and Steve automatically jumped to conclusions. It wasn't like Steve. Tim didn't express it, but he'd never felt this bad in his entire life—from being accused outright to Veronica's mental questioning of him. Tim wanted to fall into a deep sleep, but he still had other things to worry about. Liz's father slamming the front door jolted Tim back to reality.

Charles Carlough was a prominent attorney in Charleston. Out of all the teenagers' parents, he was the most conservative. He always wore suits of the finest quality, carried a briefcase around, and would occasionally smoke a pipe. Mr. Carlough was also the perpetrator when it came to Liz's constant spoiling.

The only qualities Liz seemed to have inherited from her father were his eyebrows and hair color—both dark brown. He was the only member of the Carlough family who didn't have an annoying voice. In fact, Mr. Carlough's deep voice was the polar opposite of his wife's and daughter's.

"I brought a friend! As soon as your mother said you were back, Liz, I had to pick up Stan." As Mr. Carlough approached the group in the living room, a boy with light skin and shaggy dirty-blond hair appeared behind him.

Stan Alewine wore a floral shirt underneath a blue sweater, denim jeans, and white tennis shoes. Big thick-rimmed glasses with a chestnut tint adorned his face.

"Stan?" Liz asked.

"It is me, isn't it?" Stan smirked.

"At two thirty in the morning, Dad? Really?" Liz asked, gulping at the fact that Stan was in her house. Tim was glad he wasn't Rod. Liz's current boyfriend and the guy her father wanted her to be with under one roof? Things couldn't get more problematic.

"I was over at his house, anyway. His father wanted to try me at poker." Mr. Carlough gave a small laugh. "Anyway, he's better than the hood right next to you."

The entire group shot imaginary daggers at Mr. Carlough with disgust. Mr. Carlough was outspoken, and he never hid his dislike for Rod, so he easily ignored their glares. He'd made it clear early on that he didn't care what any of them thought.

"Nice to see you too, *sir*," Rod said dully, except for the 'sir' part, which noticeably came across as sarcastic.

"Honey, his name is Rod!" Liz's mother shouted from the kitchen.

"Oh." Her father paused, his blank expression not changing. "What a *nice* name."

Mrs. Carlough rushed out of the kitchen and grabbed onto her husband's hand. One more comment, and a heated situation was bound to happen.

"I'm sorry, sweetheart. We're going to bed now. Good night, everyone." Liz's mother dragged her father upstairs and disappeared.

Stan made eye contact with everyone sitting on the couch. He ended up taking a seat on the floor, sitting midway between the couch and the television. Then it became quiet, with the exception of the television, as everyone watched him.

"Sacrifice," Tim said.

"Sacrifice," everyone but Stan said in unison.

"What on earth does that mean?" Stan asked. His cluelessness on the subject made Tim snicker. Saying sacrifice was an inside joke between him and the others. Whenever someone they didn't care for tried talking to them for some reason, someone would whisper the word. All in all, it was a stupid little thing.

"Nothing," Tim responded. "Say, you're rich—right, Stan? We've heard about you before. Do you know someone named Tammy?"

"Tammy Heston?" Stan asked. "I do. Why do you ask?"

"Wow!" Rod laughed, changing the discussion. "Moneybags gets out."

Stan smirked deviously at Rod. "Yes, my sister, my two loving parents, and I love to hang out as a family," he said.

Tim felt it was somewhat odd how literally Stan took Rod's comment.

"That's all going to go downhill," Rod said. "Family problems will come around. You'll feel like everything's coming apart, and then you'll think a legend is real and lives in the back shed of our school." He took a deep breath.

"Story...of...your...life." Alan said while he and Rod picked up their cups of hot chocolate and toasted.

"Stan! Go home!" Liz squealed, inadvertently changing the subject. "You are not needed here!"

"Wait." Stan froze in confusion. "A legend? What legend are you talking about?" Stan eyed Rod quizzically.

"The one about Ray Kuiper," Rod answered. "Have you heard of it before?"

"S'matter of fact, I have. So?" Stan asked.

"Well, when you learn about it and, all of a sudden, later that night you see weird messages placed in the old custodian shack or whatever, it makes you question everything." Rod shrugged. "Anyway, I'm over it. I just want to get wasted."

"Woo!" Tim and Steve high-fived, which gave Tim assurance that Steve must've been kidding with his careless accusations.

"There is the Rodney we know!" Richie laughed.

The two girls in the house smiled along with the others. But Veronica chuckled offhand. "Rodney?" she blurted out. "I always thought your name was Roderick."

"Come on, Veronica. Only snobs have that name," Tim said.

"My father's name is Roderick," Stan sneered.

"Tim's point exactly." Liz smiled at Tim.

Tim smiled back—not one too obvious, but just enough so that Liz saw it was on his face.

"Thanks, Richard." Rod clanged glasses with him.

"Don't forget Timothy." Veronica raised an eyebrow and looked at Tim.

"And Steven." Tim eagerly pointed to Steve.

Then all of a sudden, it seemed as though everything was back to normal. Here they were, laughing and throwing strudels at one another. Well, everyone but Stan. Stan was in the middle thinking hard about something. Tim was no mind reader, but if suspects were up for murder, Stan would have been number one.

"OK." Veronica calmed everyone down. "We leave for the lake house at four?"

"Correct," Alan replied.

"We come back next Friday?" Veronica asked.

"Yep. Earlier, though, if one of us gets knocked up." Richie laughed and looked at Liz and then Tim.

"Real funny." Tim threw a pillow at Richie, who nearly dodged it, but the pillow grazed the side of his face.

"But, guys!" Liz waved her arms in the air. "I seriously think that we shouldn't go. What if Ray Kuiper really is here? What will we do?"

"If Ray Kuiper really is here, then we get the hell out of here." Alan laughed.

"Exactly," Rod stated. "We should go somewhere far, far away."

"Who's going to pay for our plane tickets?" Veronica asked.

"Liz," Richie suggested. Liz punched him on the shoulder.

She looked pretty hot when she punched him, Tim suddenly thought. He blinked twice to get rid of the thought.

"Ow!" Richie howled. "Oh yeah, and it has to be somewhere I can find some of my mary-ja-wana."

"You mean marijuana?" Veronica inquired.

"You say 'potato'; I say 'potahto.'"

"You said 'potato' twice." Tim smiled.

"Shut up." Richie buried his face in the pillow, smiling.

"It has to be someplace far away and someplace with weed," Veronica whispered. "Let's go to Mexico."

"Ha-ha!" Stan laughed. "If a murderer is on the loose, what makes you think he doesn't already have the equipment to hunt you guys down? If he saw you, he's after you—easy as that."

The group had all eyes back on Stan for a second. He was smirking at them like he was waiting for them to ask more questions.

"Well, he does have a point," Tim whispered.

"My eyes hurt," Liz complained.

"Then go to sleep, babe." Rod put his arms around her as she laid her head on his shoulder, closing her eyes.

"Well, what would you do, rich boy?" Richie popped his head up from the pillow, placing the cushion behind his back.

"Do what I call a *run*." Stan pointed at them all and said, "Runners."

"What the hell is a runner?" Veronica questioned.

"Runners defeat the killer. Always." Rod spoke for Stan before looking at him, his expression turning into a scowl. "I know where you're going with this, Stan," Rod stated. "I don't like it."

"Easy." Stan ignored him and answered Veronica. "Out of the five of you, I assume two or three of you will come out dead. Based on your weakness, guy with glasses"—he pointed to Tim—"I think you might be the first kill."

"OK, asshole." Tim rolled his eyes.

"Runners set up the trap for the killer and then run." Stan's smirk grew bigger. "Runners defeat the killer—always."

Then he got up and walked into the kitchen. Tim could've sworn he heard Stan call them "suckers" under his breath. Once Stan was gone, it seemed like the room got warmer, as if Stan's presence was malevolent.

"That guy is freaky," Tim whispered. "I think he's a killer in his own way."

"I agree," Liz whispered, nowhere near falling asleep as her eyes fluttered open. All of a sudden, she turned enthusiastic, removing her head from Rod's shoulder. "Guys, guess what is almost here?" she shouted.

All but Rod covered their ears in order to protect their eardrums before Liz's screaming made them burst.

"Our deaths?" Richie asked, trying very hard to keep his cool as he rubbed his ears.

"No! Yes—no! My birthday! Tuesday is my birthday!" Liz beamed.

"No kidding!" Richie feigned a laugh. "Shut up."

"Hey, screw off." Rod rose up from the couch and glared at Richie. "I hate the way you guys talk to Liz like she's some type of little girl!"

"She is a year younger than all of us, so to me, she is still just a child. But who am I to talk? I'm a child at heart." Veronica smiled.

"Richie, Alan, and Steve," Rod corrected, "you guys had better get it together, because Liz is going to be with us for a while."

"That's what Alan said about Sam." Richie pointed over at Alan, snickering.

"Oh, Samantha," Alan groaned. "She was nice."

"Yeah, asshole, and I never treated Sam with anything but respect," Rod sneered.

"Sam was not an annoying rich girl," Steve corrected.

Rod rolled his eyes and sat down next Liz again. "Whatever," he said, shaking his head.

"Anyway, Sam and Alan really broke up because"—Richie cackled—"she's a lesbian."

"Ha." Tim chuckled. "That's what caused you to break up with her? I don't know about you, but..." Tim paused and looked at Veronica. Tim gathered he may have been speaking more than he should have.

"Mhmm?" Veronica smiled questionably.

"Nah, we were just arguing so much." Alan's voice fell. "But it's fine. Anyway, who the hell are you to talk about lesbians, Richie? You said the exact same thing about Natasha Athene, and what happened? You two ended up dating!"

A classic example of thinking before speaking. Richie conceded defeat right then and there, taking a bite of his strudel. The funny thing was—the two were still together, but Natasha had been in Spain for the past four months as part of a school program. He quickly decided to change the subject back to what everyone in the room was really thinking about, whether consciously or not.

"What did Stan mean about runners?" Richie's voice sounded less enthusiastic than before.

"I don't know—but I think we should find out," Tim answered, speaking on behalf of the rest of the group, who didn't know what to say.

7

THE IDEAL

"Elizabeth!" Mrs. Carlough yelled, the first words spoken all morning.

Tim opened his eyes and wandered around in a complete daze. He realized he'd never taken his glasses off, a sign of how tired he truly had been the night before.

Tim assumed the gang had crashed around four thirty. He searched for a clock but ended up gazing at the way everyone was positioned. He'd been sleeping on the couch with Veronica cuddled up next to him. Liz and Rod were curled up on the floor, Richie was sleeping in the big chair, and Alan had his head placed on Richie's leg, his blue baseball cap covering his face. Steve, however, was nowhere to be seen. Neither was Stan.

Tim remembered his dreams vividly, and they'd been positive: the group at the lake house doing their usual immature antics in the lake, jumping into the water with no thoughts of the night before. Just thinking about the dream, Tim was able to feel as though he was back in the lake. He could feel the sunshine on his skin and hear the sounds of birds cawing. When his eyes closed, he imagined the surrealistic sight of the massive trees surrounding the lake, the sun reflecting picture-perfectly off the surface.

"What time is it?" he whispered.

"Elizabeth!" Her mother's voice rang through everyone's ears again. "Get up!" She leaned against the kitchen door. "Your father and I are about to go to work, and we'd like to see you all off!"

"What time is it?" Steve popped up from behind the couch, his question more audible than Tim's.

"It's seven thirty in the morning." Liz's father came down in a gray suit and black tie. "Elizabeth, your mother and I are off to work."

Tim groaned. He never got up this early on weekends—unless it was Christmas morning. And he was thirteen.

"Houses don't sell themselves," her mother chimed, adjusting the orange turtleneck she was wearing. For a woman in her early forties, she had a hip sense of fashion.

"Fun." Stan walked downstairs too, wearing a gray silk robe over the clothes he'd arrived in earlier in the morning.

"If we are not back by the time you leave tonight, leave a note," Mr. Carlough said as he and his wife strolled out.

The door closed, but it reopened seconds later. Mrs. Carlough popped her head inside for a brief second. "And be safe, everyone, but don't let it stop you all from having fun." With a smile, she left.

As soon as the door closed, Stan spoke first. "OK."

The group didn't budge from where they'd been resting. They were all too comfortable. Liz had furniture that was far cozier than theirs. But most of them heard Stan's voice. Remembering he was still with them made the group somewhat worried.

"Veronica, Liz, Richie, get up," Steve moaned, walking on his knees to the big chair. He shook Alan's hat in front of his face to wake him.

"You guys will be the runners this afternoon. Don't be scared." Stan smiled and sat down near Tim's feet.

"I had a nightmare that a rich asshole was invading our conversation last night, guys." Alan popped his head up, pushing up his cap along the way. Then he looked at Stan and grinned. "That's the guy!" He pointed.

"Thanks, fucker. Now, if you don't mind being the first runner." Stan smiled sleazily in return.

"What the hell is a runner?" Veronica stretched and sat up, letting Tim's hands slide onto her waist.

"I don't know," Tim whispered. He'd forgotten the entire conversation they'd had earlier. He was still zoned out, for the most part.

"It's an ideal thing, really," Stan continued, leaning against the television, which was currently off. "For instance, Baseball Cap will walk outside and go into the woods. Go fishing—who cares. The killer will come try to kill you, and—"

Alan interrupted. "I run?"

"No. While the killer is after you, Glasses, shall we say, will jump behind the killer and grab his neck, fighting until…you run."

"Who the hell taught you this bullcrap?" Liz tiredly cuddled up with Rod.

"It's from a movie," Stan said.

Everyone who was awake enough filled the room with groans and jeers. Alan threw a pillow at Stan, who let it strike him. If he'd moved, an expensive golden vase would've been the victim. That didn't stop Richie from throwing a pillow of his own, which hit Stan in the stomach.

"Get outta here!" Richie yelled.

"Go home already," Tim said between yawns.

"Fine. I'll leave right now." Stan got up, removing the robe and tossing it at Alan.

"Finally," Liz whispered.

"But don't be surprised if you find my body somewhere because you guys kicked me out at this early hour—and on my hand, the saying 'I have a secret to tell' written in blood. Ever heard that story before, Rod?" Then he smiled, laughed to himself, and walked down the hallway, leaving the house.

"Creepy fucker," Alan quipped as he tossed the robe onto the floor. Veronica chuckled.

"Hey, Liz," Tim said. *Damn, I meant Veronica. Play it off. Play it off.*

"Yes?" She looked up from Rod's chest and smiled.

"I—I—um…actually, this is to everyone." Tim cleared his throat. "We break to my house for breakfast in a couple of minutes. Someplace Stan and this killer won't be."

"Good." Richie nodded.

"Then we go to get lunch later, then pack, and then, well"—Tim bit his lip—"that's it."

Crap! All my friends near my parents. Dammit! I told them I was going to be home again for my suitcases, and instead I'm bringing the whole pack there. This is dangerous.

"OK." Veronica laughed again, putting her hands on Tim's.

"And Veronica." Tim rose up, wrapping his arms around her waist, Veronica's perfect eyes meeting his.

"Yes, Tim?" Veronica asked.

"I have a present for you. Today is our two-year-and-one-month anniversary." Tim smiled proudly.

"And what did you get me?" she teased, close to blushing.

"It's at my house. It's a record that you've been wanting for a while," Tim replied.

"Awesome!" Alan interjected into Tim and Veronica's little moment. "Let's go to Tim's house and listen to it!"

"Um, my present—no." Veronica giggled. "But I'm sure Tim's father has another record you can listen to."

"Unless the Bee Gees have a *Murder on the Rise* album, I think not," Richie mumbled. Steve mimicked a gagging face at the mention of the world's biggest disco act. "Otherwise, I say after Tim's we hit up Subway."

"No! Frankie's Pizza and Pasta. I heard that new Italian joint is supposed to be off the charts." Veronica smiled.

"Ew! Grease!" Liz squealed.

"Five Dollar Burger," Rod pitched in.

"Let's just hurry up. The faster we pace things, the sooner we'll be out of here." Tim adjusted his glasses—for the first time that morning.

Alan's eyes grew large, as though he had just seen an eclipse.

"Timothy adjusted his glasses," Alan said.

"For a statement, that wasn't even that smart!" Richie cackled. Alan ended up laughing as well.

"You know, sometimes I think you guys are gay." Steve raised an eyebrow. "But I know of your escapades; you've both had your gal pals, especially when you all go to those ridiculous disco clubs, which disputes my other theory of gay."

"Gay—wow," Liz said in shock. "Don't see many of them these days."

"You never know what'll happen in the future." Tim smiled at Liz. "But I will still be straight."

"Forever and always." Veronica cleared her throat.

Uh-oh, Tim thought. *She saw me smile at Liz. It was only in a friendly way! Veronica can't think I actually have the hots for Liz, can she? I mean, for Pete's sake, Elizabeth Carlough isn't Veronica Leeds!*

Tim stared at Veronica, trying to find something to say.

"Wow," she mouthed to him and rolled her eyes, removing herself from his grip and getting off the couch.

"It's not like that," Tim accidentally said out loud.

Then all eyes were on him once again for what felt like the millionth time this weekend. *Crap.* Tim noticed Steve cross his arms and shake his head at him.

"What? You and Liz? It looks like it with all this smiling," Veronica jeered. "I don't have time for my feelings to be played with." She glared scornfully at Liz, who whimpered. "So you pick now," Veronica continued, "me or her."

"Veronica, don't you think you might be going a little overboard?" Rod countered, lifting himself from the ground and out of Liz's grip. "It's just smiling, and I'm actually glad Tim has decided to be kind to Liz for once."

"Yeah," Liz said softly. "I wouldn't do anything to get between you and Tim."

Veronica's face said she wasn't buying it. She grabbed Liz by her sweater and moved closer to her, her expression hardening.

"Tell me you don't like Tim." Veronica's tone got higher. "Tell me!"

"Ease off, Veronica," Rod demanded.

Liz opened her mouth to say something but then closed it and looked to the floor.

"You like him, don't you?" Veronica glared furiously. "You're pathetic."

"No, I don't." Liz popped her head back up. "You know I love Rod. And I'm not the kind of person who would do something like that."

"Better not be," Veronica added. "Or your pretty face will meet my pretty fist." Veronica got even closer to Liz, clenching a fist and putting it in front of Liz's face. "Don't think I'm kidding either."

"G-g-got it." Liz trembled.

"And you"—Veronica smiled coldly at Tim, whose heart began to palpitate violently—"choose your bait before you fish. I would hate for you to pick me and then leave me for the fishes to eat."

"Isn't that what bait's for?" Alan asked. Though nervous, Tim couldn't help but smile.

Veronica spun around to Alan with a look that could only be interpreted as "You're asking—no, *begging*—for trouble."

"You want to meet my foot, don't you? My foot said your ass could use some kicking," Veronica sneered as she bopped Alan's cap, knocking it in front of his face.

"Let's get back on topic. No need for animosity—right, everyone?" Richie jumped from the couch and in front of Alan quickly. "Five Dollar Burger or Frankie's?"

"Frankie's," Liz stated. She probably was trying to appease Veronica in some way.

"Agreed," Veronica said emotionlessly. "Frankie's. Amen." Then she got up and stormed out the door.

"It's seven forty-five in the morning," Alan moaned. "Do we have to leave now?"

"Yes, before your ass gets a kicking." Steve laughed, pushing Alan to the door as the rest of them walked outside into the frosty-cold air of day-breaking Charleston.

They walked down the sidewalk. Anyone who noticed them would have sensed nothing but tension; they were spread out as though they were all trying to get somewhere with strangers blocking their every move.

Tim admitted to himself that he'd been a fool before, and this only brought his self-esteem lower. As much as he thought Liz was a little attractive, he still knew—he damn well knew—that Veronica was the right one for him. He'd known from the moment he first kissed her after bringing her home from their first date.

They had seen *Airport '77*, and the movie ended up being better than the two had expected. They'd walked to Veronica's house hand in hand as the skies dimmed. Upon reaching her door, the two were about to part when suddenly, as if on an urge, Tim leaned in and stole a kiss.

Something about her reaction told Tim she'd been taken by surprise, but to him, the remainder of the kiss was like an electrical charge from a plug slamming into an outlet.

Tim would never forget that day, yet here they were walking side by side but not saying a word to each other. Alan, Steve, and Richie were behind them, with Rod in the back. Liz was chasing after them, having had to find the house key and lock the door.

The entire way to his house, all Tim did was observe his girlfriend. From her long black hair, to her large blue eyes that were lidded with mildly dark eye shadow, to the way she paced down the sidewalk as if provoked. Tim cleared his throat to at least say something to the girl he cared so much about, but he couldn't bring himself to mutter a word. Veronica's hastening speed did nothing to help him.

"Am I man or fool?" Tim mumbled under his breath in disappointment as he eyed his girlfriend marching before him.

Everyone soon arrived at Tim's house. Tim fished his keys out of his loose pajama pockets. He unlocked the door and opened it slowly, just in case his parents were in the living room.

He let himself inside first, and the others followed. Tim's parents were nowhere to be seen. The television was off, and so were the lights. The rising sun outside illuminated the room.

"You guys can chill down here and do whatever you want. I'll be right back." Tim trudged upstairs, somewhat glad to be away from his friends for the moment.

He entered his room, unchanged from the day before. Going into his closet, Tim retrieved a square item enfolded in wrapping paper with cartoon turkeys decorating it. A record, *Crossing the Red Sea with the Adverts* by the Adverts. It was his gift for Veronica—if she still wanted it, anyway.

Tim and Veronica rarely argued or fought with each other. This was a rare occurrence, and the less of it happening, the better. Maybe Veronica didn't know it, but she had a bit of a temper when she got jealous. And when it occasionally came out, it was intense.

Tim lay back on his bed to relax and found a note stuck to the edge of his nightstand. It was from his parents, and it said that they were out and would be back by noon. Satisfied, Tim realized he didn't want to leave his room. To him, there was no need to get up when all that was downstairs was trouble. Besides, he couldn't face Veronica. Not now, at least.

Tim had never felt this distance from Veronica before, and he never thought he would. He wasn't going back downstairs unless someone wanted him, and even then, he'd be reluctant. At the very least, he was content with being away from the strain of dealing with the rest of the group for the time being.

Crossing the Red Sea with the Adverts lying on his chest, Tim stared at his ceiling, the fan swirling above him. The door creaked opened, but Tim's eyes remained focused on the ceiling. It was Veronica. Closing the door behind her, she took a seat by Tim's stomach. He remained motionless.

"Tim?"

"Yeah?"

"Listen. I want to apologize for what happened at Liz's. I shouldn't have gotten all upset like that. I—I just got scared. I felt as though I was inches away from losing you." Her mouth quivered. "I felt—I felt as though I'd end up like my mother once Dad left her…"

Tim rose, the record sliding from his stomach to his thighs, and put his hands on Veronica's shoulders. Her eyes were closed, the wild black hair partly obscuring her face. Tim could feel her body quaking.

"That's totally understandable, Veronica. But listen to me now—and good. I would never cheat on you. Not with Liz, not with anyone. You're perfect—everything about you is. If I ever lost you, I wouldn't be able to function." Tim moved a hand to Veronica's cheek and gently brought her face in front of his. She managed to look at him in the eyes, moving a few tufts of his brown hair out from in front of his glasses.

"I feel the same way, Tim. I guess it's the way you look at her."

"After being forced to spend time with her in the woods last night, she's not as superficial as everyone thinks. I may be in the minority, but she at least deserves some respect." Tim used his free hand to grab the record from his thigh. "But no more about Liz, instead, I have a present for you." He handed it to her, removing the other hand from her cheek.

Veronica smiled. She tore up the wrapping paper in seconds. The moment the sea of multiple swirling colors on the cover struck her, her face lit up. This sight brought a smile to Tim's face, the first true smile he had donned the entire morning.

"*Crossing the Red Sea with the Adverts!* Oh, Tim, I love you so much." Veronica beamed brightly.

"I love you so much even more." Tim grinned and hugged her tightly.

Tim slowly moved his head and pressed his lips gently on Veronica's soft neck. He continued as she bit her bottom lip. His lips soon relocated up her neck to her chin and her cheeks until he reached her lips.

Veronica placed the record toward the end of the bed as she wrapped her arms around Tim's neck. He grabbed her in his arms and laid her under his body. They continued kissing as Tim began to squeeze Veronica's hips gently.

This was the first time the couple had been alone in a week. The day before hadn't counted, in Tim's opinion. The two had barely kissed each other, and Tim's parents had been downstairs. It felt like it had been forever, but now it was worth it.

But not all good things last without something barging in. In this case, their romantic moment was interrupted by Tim's door bursting open.

"What's taking you guys so long?" Alan asked.

He saw Tim and Veronica and turned red as he looked back toward the door. "Oh."

"Now I feel like Steve," Tim whispered into Veronica's neck. She giggled.

"Well, I came here to let you both know Steve and I are cooking up some pancakes." Alan backed up slowly.

"Sounds good. Take your time." Veronica lifted up her available hand.

"Will do." Alan smiled sheepishly as he walked out the door, closing it behind him.

"That was close. I wanna do more, but when you're in a house with the likes of Alan and Richie…" Veronica said.

"Agreed." Tim snickered.

Tim lifted himself, albeit reluctantly, off Veronica and from his bed, but not before stealing a kiss from his girlfriend. He walked out of his bedroom and found the entire downstairs smelling like batter from the pancakes on the stove.

Veronica followed after, and the two sat on the couch together. Tim wrapped an arm around his girlfriend. Alan and Steve were cooking in the kitchen, flipping the pancakes with spatulas. Richie was sitting to the left of Tim and Veronica in Tim's father's favorite recliner.

"Where's Rod and Liz?" Veronica asked, looking around.

"Liz is in the bathroom, and Rod is outside," Richie replied. "I'm surprised you even asked, Veronica. You seemed pretty pissed off back at Liz's place, and I never would've expected you to care about their whereabouts—er, mainly Liz's."

"I guess you can say I'm feeling better now that things have cooled off." Veronica kissed Tim on the cheek, and he grinned.

"I'll be right back, lovely," Tim said. "Wanna see how Rod is doing."

Veronica nodded as Tim removed himself from the couch and headed outside. Rod was sitting on the grass, legs outstretched and arms behind him for support. He was staring into the cloudy gray sky, thinking. He hadn't blinked once; he hadn't moved an inch. Tim kneeled by Rod.

"Hey, man," Tim said.

"Hey." Rod glanced at Tim behind him. A cool breeze blew their hair slightly.

"What's going on?"

"Nothing, really. Trying to find solace, I guess." Rod shrugged. "What place is better to search than one's mind?"

"Nice analogy."

"Thanks."

"Rod," Tim said, "I'm asking you this as a friend. Do you think you can manage going on the trip to the lake house later?"

"Yeah—why?"

"With all the things going on in your life, the car accident and stuff, you just seem out of it to me. You've been staring off into space more often than usual."

"I am out of it," Rod admitted. "But going on the lake-house trip is the vacation I need. Hell, imagine what kind of time we'd have. It'd bring me out of this slump I've been in for the past few weeks."

"You've convinced me."

"Mission accomplished." Rod smiled. He began to rise, but he stopped, turning back at Tim. "And, pal, don't worry. I know you and Liz wouldn't do anything like that. I've known you for years, and you're a good guy."

"Thanks for that, man. I do appreciate it."

"Don't mention it."

"Food's ready!" Steve walked outside wearing an old apron and holding a spatula in his hand.

Rod patted Tim's shoulder, got up, and strode inside. Tim followed suit, but Steve stopped him before he could get inside.

"Everything all right between you two?" Steve questioned.

Tim nodded. "More or less. Richie and I were skeptical about whether or not Rod should go on the trip. He says he's good to go, and I want to take his word for it, but I'm still not sure he's up for it." He frowned.

"Maybe the trip is exactly what he needs right now: a getaway."

Maybe.

The two guys went inside, and Steve began to help Alan serve the breakfast. Tim entered the kitchen, and Alan handed him a plate with three pancakes.

"Damn, I didn't know you could cook." Tim inspected the food. It looked edible enough.

"You learn something new every day, my pal." Alan grinned.

Veronica and Richie were the only ones at the table. Tim took a seat between them. As Alan served Rod his pancakes, Liz headed downstairs and sat next to Veronica. Steve stood just outside the kitchen with the wall phone to his ear.

"Hey, Tammy. It's Steve. I just wanted to apologize for how everything turned out last night…We got bored all of a sudden—didn't really feel like staying the entire night. Besides, did you actually think I could manage to spend the rest of the night there without you?…It's true, and thank you for understanding; it means more than a lot… Yeah, we're still heading to the lake house today. Why?…You can? That's great! We're heading out from Tim's place at four. You know where he lives?…Even better. Sounds great, baby. I'll see you then. Bye."

The moment Steve entered the kitchen, he appeared to be on the exuberant cloud nine. By the looks of it, the expression of contentment on his face wasn't leaving anytime soon. He took a seat next to Rod while Richie spoke between pancake bites.

"Guys, around two thirty we should all go back to our places and get packed and ready and meet back at Tim's before four. Then we can go," Richie remarked, rising up to get the orange juice out of the fridge.

"Sounds good. Whose car are we taking?" Steve served himself two pancakes.

"Only Veronica and Rod have cars that can fit all seven of us," Alan pointed out.

"And my car needs repairs." Rod sighed, trying not to think about the accident. Any remembrance made Rod's head throb.

"Yeah, about the seven of us…" Steve began.

"What is it, Steve?" Tim cocked an eyebrow.

Steve took a deep breath. The saying "If you can't stand the heat, get out of the kitchen" was about to run wild in this here kitchen. "I was just speaking to Tammy on the phone—"

"You didn't dare, Steve!" Liz glared viciously at him.

"Oh no." Veronica placed a hand on her forehead.

"She asked me if she could come along to the lake house with us, and I sorta told her that, yes, she could." Steve nervously scratched the back of his neck.

Sighs, complaints, and annoyance filled the kitchen faster than an out-of-control forest fire. As if it weren't bad enough that Steve hadn't asked the others first, the fact that it was *Tammy* he invited was the syrup on the pancake.

"Fuck no. I'm not gonna have my vacation ruined by having a slut come along with us," Liz lamented.

"Well, she's going regardless what you say," Steve retorted.

As an argument seemed to be brewing, Alan stood up at the table. His family owned the lake house; therefore, he made the final decision—whether anyone liked it or not. Before Liz could answer Steve, Alan's calm voice shocked the entire room. It was so calm that Tim felt the hairs on his arms stand up.

"She can come."

Liz glowered at Alan. She exhaled briefly, closing her eyes as she shook her head wildly. Alan's answer to the next question would let Liz decide if she'd cool down or strangle him. "What do you mean?" she complained behind clenched teeth.

"Let's just make Steve happy, OK?" Alan's voice, still calm, had a stern quality to it. "We're going to *my* lake house, so if Steve wants to invite someone, I allow it."

Liz tightened her fists and slammed them on the table, almost spilling Veronica's milk onto her. She jumped up from the table and flipped Alan off.

"Fuck Steve!" she screamed. "Fuck Steve and Tammy!"

"Shut your goddamned mouth, you psycho bitch!" Steve lost his cool and scowled at Liz.

"Chill out!" Tim yelled.

"You chill out, you asshole!" Liz screamed back, raising her hand as if she was going to slap Tim.

"Would you please mellow out, Liz?" Richie groaned. The screaming affected him less, compared to the others. "I mean, damn, you're so fucking annoying sometimes!"

There was no way Liz was going to win the argument. Pouting her lips and crossing her arms, she took a seat. Steve ran his fingers through his wavy hair and left the kitchen to cool off.

But Steve's words had caused Rod to rush up from the table, grab Steve by his T-shirt, and slam him into the wall. Rod had learned to take Richie's "bitch" comments in stride, but Steve calling Liz a "psycho bitch" was crossing the line by far. No one said anything for a few moments. A cloud of hostility seemed to hover over the group.

"Steve, I'm not playing around. Stop treating my girlfriend like trash. Don't ever call Liz a psycho bitch again, all right? I'm sick and tired of hearing my girlfriend referred to as a bitch. She's not a damn bitch," Rod sneered.

Steve glowered at Rod, not acknowledging him at all. Tensions had finally risen to an all-time high among the group. Tim was wondering whether or not they'd be able to leave intact. It seemed to be only a matter of time before one of them would call it quits and refuse to go on the trip.

"I'm sorry."

Rod looked Steve directly in the eyes as he let go of his shirt. He went back to the table and began a conversation as if nothing had just occurred. Steve, whose forehead sported a thin strip of sweat, rashly left the kitchen and sat on the couch.

"Well, that's eight people, and none of us has a car that can fit eight," Rod said.

"S-Stan's car can," Liz suggested.

"But do you really want Stan coming along?" Veronica asked.

"We're not settling for that." Tim sighed. It hurt him to say that to Liz, but it was best.

The last thing anyone wanted was to have Stan join them on the trip. His first impression was that Stan was a creeper. Once he was exiled from Liz's house, that was it. Tim wished to have nothing more to do with Stan. His addition would only bring unwanted anxiety. Tammy was more than enough.

"I have an alternative." Veronica's voice rang through the house.

"What?" Alan asked, his voice tinged with hope.

"A Winnebago!" Steve burst through the doors before Veronica could even share what she had to say. It didn't matter now.

"One of those drivable houses?" Alan raised his eyebrows.

"Yeah! You see—we're in luck. My brother's back from college for the next two weeks, and he owns one of them. He would be happy to let us borrow it for the vacation. His Winnebago has a driver's seat, a passenger's seat, two couches—one of which can fit three people; the other, two—a lounge chair, a fridge, a bathroom, and a bed."

A stellar idea. The perfect choice, the perfect timing. Steve had the answer to everyone's prayers. But there was one problem barricading them. A big one.

"Steve, you are a practical lifesaver, but you still need to get his permission." Richie sighed as he rose from the table to take some dishes to the sink.

"Let me call him, and you'll see." Steve went back to the phone.

"And what if he doesn't? What are we going to do then?" Veronica asked. "My suggestion would've been taking a bus, but that doesn't sound too fun, does it?"

"Take separate cars, I guess." Tim shrugged, taking a bite of his pancakes.

"Damn. I was hoping for it to be like a road trip, all of us shoved into the car together." Veronica frowned.

"Just keep your hopes up, love." Tim kissed Veronica's forehead.

With breakfast over, the majority of the group left the kitchen and entered the living room. Richie continued doing dishes while Liz remained seated, her face buried in open palms. Rod was with her, comforting her.

Sitting in the middle of the couch, Tim grabbed the remote from the crease between the cushions and flipped the television on. It was on ABC, and the *Plastic Man* cartoon was about to come on. Alan jumped over the couch and landed at Tim's right, grabbing the remote control and turning the volume up.

Alan didn't care that he was a senior in high school; he loved Saturday-morning cartoons. Veronica was sitting to the left of Tim, and she didn't mind, even though she wanted twelve thirty to roll around so she could watch *American Bandstand*.

"Good news, everyone." Steve placed the phone back on the hook. He ran in front of the television, almost tripping over his own feet from enthusiasm. "My brother said we can borrow the Winnebago!"

"My man!" Alan jumped off the couch and high-fived Steve hard enough to make Steve wince. He instantly grabbed his reddening hand in pain. Alan grabbed his cap from his head and howled in excitement. All he needed was Samantha Garfield, and Alan would've fainted from the excitement.

Everyone else—sans Liz, who Rod was still trying to cheer up—was reassured that the plans were still going on. Nothing was going to stop them. Nor was anyone, namely Tammy, going to hold them back. All in all, it was up to Steve to keep her in line. If Tammy didn't start anything with Liz, that would be a piece of cake.

"This is going to be so rad." Veronica beamed. "I have butterflies in my stomach; I'm that excited."

"Now." Steve smiled boldly as he sat down on the couch, taking Alan's seat in the process. "Let's get this *Plastic Man* show on the road!"

As Alan sat in the recliner, Veronica looked up at her boyfriend. "Hey, Tim, do you and Rod still have that thing planned for Liz and me?"

"Without a doubt, my sweet love," Tim replied.

With that, heroic music began to play on the television. Alan and Steve were at the edges of their seats. To Tim's and Veronica's amusement, they spoke along with the opening in unison: "From out of the pages of DC Comics comes the world's newest and greatest superhero"—Alan and Steve looked at each other—"Plastic Man!"

"Oh brother," Tim remarked.

Time went by as laughter echoed throughout Tim's house. Finally—it had taken long enough, but finally—there was peace.

8

OCCURRENCES

It was noon—possibly a bit after. Steve awoke from a nap he unknowingly had fallen into. Considering the lack of sleep he'd gotten at Liz's, it was no surprise to him that he'd dozed off again. His couch was also more comfortable than the floor he'd slept on at Liz's house. Maybe it was just the fact that he was used to this old one. Everyone, including him, had left Tim's around eleven thirty to get ready. Steve had been a bit fretful about their leaving, considering an alleged killer was lurking around Charleston, but the fact that they left in a group helped put his fears to rest. Plus, his friends' houses were all close together.

Steve found this to be the best time to rid himself of the clothes he had been wearing since the night before. His boat shoes had old dirt built up on the soles, and his black pajama pants had some dirt stains at the hems. His favorite shirt was devoid of any marks. Steve rose from the couch and stretched, cracking his back in the process. It was a good feeling, reenergizing even.

Steve noticed that the house smelled of vanilla (thanks to Air Wick) as he dragged his feet out the living room and down the hallway to the bathroom. His parents were going to be back at any minute, so a shower would awaken him even further, preparing him to answer the questions his parents were bound to ask.

"You're still here?" he imagined them asking. "We thought you'd be gone by now." Steve loved his parents, but their questions could go on and on for hours. To make matters worse, they'd also probably complain about his friends, specifically Alan and Richie. Mr. and Mrs. Waisner had doubts about "those two goons." Steve's parents had known Tim, Rod, and Veronica since they were young children—Steve had attended kindergarten with them—but Alan's and Richie's constant antics were a bit much for Steve's parents to handle.

Steve's mother's reservations stemmed from the time Alan and Richie had stayed the night at Steve's place in sixth grade. Not only did they hoard the food from the refrigerator, but they constantly watched the television at a high volume. Then Alan accidently forgot to pick up his marbles from the staircase before going to bed. When Richie woke up late at night to get some milk, evading the marbles that he knew were there, the sounds of him slamming the fridge door shut were loud enough for Steve's mother to go downstairs and check. She, however, *didn't* know about the marbles, and, well, it was a sight to behold.

But Steve was alone in the house for the time being and wouldn't have to worry about his mother agonizing over Alan and Richie. And what about him? It would've been worse if Steve was still wearing those dirty clothes and lounging about. They surely would've questioned what Steve had been up to at the sleepover. Steve knew that if they asked about it, he'd have to make something up. He'd be out of his mind to tell his parents they found weird messages at the school. And that he had sex there too.

If anything, Steve was tempted to ask his parents about Ray Kuiper. They'd been in the same graduating class as Kuiper; surely they would know about him and the events surrounding his supposed death. What's more, they could've even known him.

As Steve asked himself question after question, the peppermint scent of his bathroom drowned out the smell of vanilla. He rubbed his eyes for a few seconds, trying to rid them of the image of the carving inside the shed. It'd been lingering in his mind the entire day, even intruding in his dreams.

Steve splashed warm water on his face and gazed into the mirror. His black bangs dropped just over his eyes. "What's even real anymore?" Steve asked himself aloud. "I'll never know."

He turned the shower on. If he needed anything right now, it was this—and Tammy joining him, but that was another case. As the warm water flowed through the showerhead, Steve stripped out of his clothes and stepped into the tub.

Almost immediately, every feeling of tiredness was out of his system. Steve stood directly under the water, his wavy hair dangling in front of his face. His eyes closed, panoramas of memories shifting into thoughts about what was going down for the remainder of the day.

Sooner or later, everyone would be back at Tim's place. This included Tammy, but Steve figured that if his friends didn't start anything with her, there was no reason for her to stir up trouble. Only he could keep an eye on her.

Steve snapped out of his reverie when the water suddenly turned cold. He almost jumped out of the shower. Shivering, he pushed the lever toward hot, but the water didn't flow warmly until the lever could go no more.

Lying plumber...

Steve spent the rest of the shower conditioning his hair and cleaning up before he got out. Wrapping a towel around himself, he grabbed his pajamas, exited the bathroom, and went into his room.

Steve dressed quickly, throwing on his boxers, socks, a pair of blue bell-bottoms, and a long-sleeved white shirt with orange sleeves. Looking under his bed, he found his favorite green Converse sneakers. He sat down on the bed and slid the shoes on.

Now he had to pack. Steve ran around his room, rapidly scavenging a week's worth of clothes and tossing everything onto the bed. He put it all into his black suitcase, which he'd pulled from the closet. Brushing his teeth, freshening himself up, and blow-drying his hair were the last few things Steve had to do. He looked in the mirror and shrugged.

"Could be worse."

Tossing the wet towel over the shower rod, Steve grabbed his suitcase and stepped out of his room. He took one more glance back at everything he was leaving behind for the week. Then his eyes focused on his father's study across the hall. Steve vividly remembered that when he was in tenth grade, his father had found his senior yearbook in the garage and placed it on the bookshelf. It hadn't mattered much to Steve then, but now he was much more interested.

Steve went into the study and found the bookshelf in the far-right corner of the room. He scanned the spine of each and every book until he found it. On the bottom shelf: *Franklin Pierce High School, Class of 1952*. Steve pulled the yearbook out of its place and investigated the pages. He figured that maybe he'd find something—maybe nothing. Either way, he'd never know unless he tried.

Steve stopped almost before he'd even begun his search. The second page was filled with signings from other classmates, including one from Tim's father, Albert Ridges. Steve couldn't believe what Tim's father had written.

"Hope the University of Michigan is fun," Steve read aloud. "Keep in touch. I'll let you know if Ray comes back. You two are my buds for life."

Steve closed the yearbook and rushed out of the room. This was crazy—no, insane. He had to let Tim know about this immediately. Hopefully his dad wouldn't mind the yearbook being gone for the week. Grabbing his suitcase and the keys to the Winnebago, Steve left his house and bolted over to his brother's camper.

Sitting in the driver's seat of the Winnebago, Steve realized this was the first time he had ever set foot in his older brother's drivable home. It was enormous and practically new, and he treated it with care as he backed out of the driveway slowly before going down the road.

Tim's gonna freak; everyone's gonna freak, Steve thought. *Discovery of a lifetime.*

Though it seemed to take forever to get to his friend's house, in actuality it wasn't long until the Winnebago was in Tim's driveway and parked next to the 1979 Pontiac Trans Am. Steve hopped out of the vehicle and dashed to Tim's front door, holding on to the yearbook tightly. He knocked on the door.

Before long, Tim opened the door. He wore a red-and-yellow-checkered shirt, blue bell-bottoms, and black boots.

"Hey, man, anyone else here yet?" Steve asked.

"Nope, you're the first one, buddy."

"Cool. Are you doing anything important?"

"Just looking for a record in the record boxes." Tim pointed to a brown box with the name Tim written on it with big bold letters. "Why?"

"You're not gonna fucking believe this."

Steve made his way inside the house and hurriedly jumped onto the couch, setting the yearbook on his lap.

"Is that the fifty-two yearbook?" Tim asked. "Hate to break it to you, Steve, but Liz and I already looked through it. We saw Ray Kuiper's picture in it."

"Bet you didn't see this in the school's yearbook."

Steve opened the yearbook to the second page as Tim sat down next to him. He pointed directly at the words he'd read minutes ago. Tim stared at the writing, scanning it. Soon he leaned away, speechless.

"Words written by your dad, to my dad, about Ray fucking Kuiper."

"Steve, if only you were here not even five minutes ago with this. My parents stopped by for a bit, and I completely forgot to ask them about Kuiper."

"Shit, really?" Steve groaned.

Tim nodded. "But keep this here. Maybe I'll give my parents a call tonight if I'm not busy with Veronica. I just don't believe it."

"Tell me about it." Steve closed the yearbook and set it on the floor. "Not only did our fathers go to school with this guy, but they knew him and were friends with him."

Tim got up from the couch and went over to the front door. "Could you show me the Winnebago? I gotta get my mind off what I just read."

"Yeah, of course."

Steve rose and opened the front door, walking outside with Tim following. The 1979 Winnebago Brave, brand-new, remained in the driveway. It was off-white with blue detailing. Hazel detailing overriding the blue made up the colors of the *W* symbols on the sides. Tim raised his eyebrows. "Damn..." was all he could say.

"A sight to be seen, huh?" Steve grinned complacently. "You can't see the inside, though, my friend. That's gonna be a surprise once all of you are here." Steve patted Tim's back, and the two friends went back inside the house. Tim began searching through his box of records.

"What record are you looking for?"

"*But the Little Girls Understand.*"

"Ah, a little Knack, huh?"

"What can I say? I'm, like, the only person who doesn't think 'My Sharona' is overplayed."

"Add me to the list; anything beats the crap the mainstreamers like." Steve took a seat back on the couch, his eyes focused on the yearbook for a few seconds. "It kills me that stuff like Aerosmith is barely on the radio nowadays yet crap like the Bee Gees and Donna Summer fills the airwaves."

Tim gave up his search for a brief second. He turned away from the boxes and to his friend. Steve slouched a bit and picked up the yearbook again, examining it carefully.

"Steve, I have a question."

"Shoot."

"Honestly, why do you think I have something for Liz? I mean, take the sleepover, for instance. You jumped immediately to conclusions just because we smiled at each other. What's the deal?"

Steve had stopped his examination of the yearbook as soon as Tim finished his first sentence. He leaned forward toward Tim and flipped his bangs from in front of his eyes. "When someone can't stand a person around their friends but smiles and seemingly gets along with that person while alone, you can only assume."

"What if I told you that while Liz and I were in the woods last night, we got to know each other a little better?"

"Last night, I would've thought you were hiding something from me. But now I understand. I will admit I was out of line with some of the accusations, and I apologize, man. I guess I just don't wanna see you or Veronica get hurt. I've known the two of you since kindergarten, for Pete's sake. You both mean a lot to me," Steve said. "Besides, with Veronica's parents divorced and all, she's sorta vulnerable."

"You know I wouldn't hurt Veronica."

"I do," Steve admitted. All of a sudden, he started smiling. "God, I hate how serious we're always acting nowadays, man. We're teenagers! We're seniors! We're about to go to a lake house for a wild week—not a business trip!"

Steve jumped up from the couch. Tim did the same from the floor. The two friends whooped as they raised their fists in the air. Another knock came at the door. Energized, Tim and Steve swung it open.

"Alan!" the two guys exclaimed.

Alan nearly fell over from the surprise. "What's got you two rejuvenated all of a sudden?" Alan laughed. He wore a blue polo and a worn-out leather jacket with dark jeans and gray Nikes along with his blue baseball cap. In his hand was a burnt-red suitcase.

"The fact that we're teenagers and we're gonna have the wildest time this weekend!" Tim exclaimed.

"Right on!" Alan grinned. "Loud music, hard alcohol, loose women, and—damn, I'm getting goose bumps! This is gonna be the life."

"Keep the loose women for yourself, pal," Steve joked. "Speaking of which, I want to thank you for allowing Tammy to come with us, Alan. I more than appreciate it."

"What are friends for?" Alan smiled. "I can dig it if you wanna invite some babes. Oh, and by the way, that Winnebago is colossal!"

Veronica and Richie were the next to arrive. Their opposite styles were humorous. She appeared ready for a Ramones concert, while Richie would've be a perfect fit in a disco club. A couple of minutes later, Rod and Liz arrived, the last of the core group.

Liz appeared almost as unhappy as she had been before everyone had left, but that was mostly because of her downcast eyes. A simple smile attempted to mask it. Rod, on the other hand, wore a full smile.

With the majority of the group at the house, Steve hid the yearbook upstairs in Tim's room. He placed it on the desk, hoping he'd remember it when they returned from the lake house. Like he'd told Tim, this was a week to go crazy. Telling everyone else about this discovery would only make them more worried, more focused on Kuiper rather than their spring-break vacation. Hiding the yearbook would do more good than bad. Coming downstairs and pouring a glass of ginger ale in the kitchen, Steve found himself finally apologizing to Liz for his outburst earlier.

Immediately after he finished his request for forgiveness, Liz perked up and hugged Steve tightly, almost knocking the wind out of him. Steve laughed, feeling somewhat better deep down inside, and found himself next to Tim once more.

"Find *Get the Knack Mach II* yet?" Steve joked.

"Shut up, Steve." Tim laughed. "Those albums are equally good."

"Whatever helps you sleep at night." Steve looked at the box full of Tim's parents' records sitting next to Tim's box. "Maybe your parents have it."

Everyone else was talking about the Winnebago. It wasn't like any of them hadn't seen one before, but they'd never been in one. Steve knelt next to Tim and opened the brown box full of Tim's parents' records. Soon he held a record in his hand.

"Hey, guess what I found," Steve said, nudging his friend.

Tim slapped his forehead upon seeing the Knack inside his parents' box of records. "Why it's in there, I'd rather not know." Tim raised his eyebrows.

Liz, who was laughing at a joke Alan had told about a guy walking into a bar with a slab of asphalt, noticed the record Steve was holding up. On an impulse, she quickly rushed over to him and slapped the back of his head.

"What was that for?" Steve asked. "My apology was sincere."

"No, it's for owning that album. I hate that album!" Liz yelled.

Everyone in the room began to chuckle, much to Liz's dissatisfaction. The sight of Liz hitting Steve over a record—now they'd seen everything. But upon closely observing the record in question, Alan and Richie dropped their jaws.

"What do you mean you hate *But the Little Girls Understand*?" Alan asked incredulously.

"Have you heard the lyrics on that garbage?" Liz whined. "Fieger sings about how his 'baby' likes to get beaten."

"So?" Steve snickered, taking a long swig of his ginger ale. "It's just a song."

"Ray Kuiper talks dirty," Richie joked, making a sly grin that sent a flying pillow his way.

Alan couldn't contain his laughter as Liz turned to Richie, giving him a stone-cold glare. Before an argument—though a lighthearted one—could build up, the doorbell rang. Veronica sauntered over to the door and opened it. Tammy appeared before her, waving and smiling brightly, fully exposing her gapped front teeth.

"Guess who?" Tammy called.

Veronica dully slammed the door straight in her face. Steve nudged Veronica away before swinging the door open again. Tammy looked annoyed at first but lit up upon seeing Steve.

"Hey, baby," Steve said, making his voice sound smooth and seductive.

"Hey." Tammy gave a sultry smile as she moved closer to Steve, running a finger up and down his chest. "Are we heading out soon?"

"Very soon. We were just trying to find a record. You know *But the Little Girls Understand?*" Steve asked as he let her in.

She wore a long-sleeved white button-down shirt and blue bell-bottoms with white boots. Her hair had been feathered, and Steve could feel his body temperature rise.

"Of course. I mean, Steve"—Tammy began to whisper—"I think I need a real neat beating sometimes."

Steve tugged his collar, as if there was steam coming up from inside his shirt, while his lips grew into a devious grin.

Tammy made eye contact with Steve's friends. Veronica, Tim, and Liz were looking at her blankly—looks that could be perceived as their not wanting her to be there. Richie, Alan, and Rod were giving her neutral expressions.

"Hey, Liz, you're looking decent," Tammy remarked sarcastically as Steve craftily slid his hands into her back pockets. Tammy wasn't one to hide what she was thinking.

"Don't push me," Liz replied, turning away.

"Hey." Alan walked between the two girls. "When we go on this trip, we'll have no arguing, or else I will force you two to leave. I will throw you from the Winnebago in a heartbeat," Alan asserted.

It was the first time annoyance had actually filled Alan's voice, which also meant he was finally being serious. He had a point, though. It wouldn't be fun if Tammy and Liz were arguing the entire time.

"Freaking fine, Alan. I won't mess with the dumb bimbo," Liz said. "Just tell her to keep her tramp paws on Steve and Steve only."

"Of course." Tammy looked away, her eyes closed. "Rod's not my type, anyway."

"Every guy is your type," Liz sneered.

"Tim isn't my type." Tammy pointed at him.

"But you would screw him if he hung sausages from his ears," Liz smirked.

Tammy faked a smile at Liz, a little bit of a scowl noticeable as she put her arm around Steve, strutting away from the door with him.

"So," Tim said, "how about that record now?"

He only succeeded in receiving a glare from Liz, the sight of which caused Tammy to snicker.

"Why not? I'm down for some Knack," Rod said.

Tammy laughed some more. "You are all the most awkward bunch I've ever seen since the Village People."

"Um, how is that funny?" Alan raised an eyebrow.

"Shut up, Alan. Speaking of *you*, where's Ryan?" Tammy looked around.

"It's *Richie*," Richie stated from the couch. Brushing Tammy off, he turned to Tim. "Tim, can we leave now? We can get more done at the lake house before sundown."

The doorbell rang unexpectedly.

"Who could that be?" Tim asked. Everyone was already at his place, and there wasn't anyone else expected to arrive.

"Let me see." Rod moved past Steve and Tammy in order to open the door.

To the surprise of all, at the door was Liz's father. He wore the same suit he'd had on that morning. Charles Carlough stared awkwardly at his daughter's boyfriend. Rod could only respond the same way.

"Mr. Carlough?" Rod began. "What happens to bring you here?"

"Daddy?" Liz looked over at her father along with the others.

"I was at work, and a bad feeling was ringing in my mind. I was just thinking that if my daughter is going to this lake house, she needs someone who can protect her," Mr. Carlough stated.

"Mr. Carlough, you can count on me. Liz is in safe hands," Rod tried his best to assure him. "Besides, if this 'protector' is Stan, then could you please tell him his *services* aren't necessary? We didn't invite him; it'd seem like a hassle."

Mr. Carlough inhaled steadily and gazed upward for a second. He glanced back at Rod sourly. Steve had seen Mr. Carlough make this face at Rod before. It pretty much read as though he had, in his words, better things to be doing than speaking with Rod. It would demean him, getting into a conversation with someone of a lower status, even though Rod also came from a well-to-do family. To Mr. Carlough, the Grandts' level wasn't enough to satisfy. And thinking of all that made Steve sick.

"Look, Todd. I don't want my daughter going to a lake house with all these guys who I know nothing about. She needs someone to protect her," Mr. Carlough stated, clearly more aggravated.

"Gee, thanks." Veronica rolled her eyes and walked into the kitchen.

"Mr. Carlough, we're Liz's friends." Rod's voice slightly but noticeably changed, as if he was struggling to keep his composure.

"Fact of the matter is, her mother may trust you all, but I don't," Mr. Carlough responded.

Liz appeared behind Rod. She asked her father what he was doing there. His answer was loud and clear. "Bringing Stan over to come on your vacation."

"Please don't!" Liz begged. "Please, please. You can trust these guys. And Veronica is going too!"

"I'm sorry, but I don't trust these boys. You need him as much as he needs you," Mr. Carlough said.

Tim and Steve slowly exchanged uncomfortable, speechless expressions. *What?* Steve thought. What did Mr. Carlough see in Stan? And what he'd said basically made it seem like he thought his daughter was soul mates with Stan.

"Daddy!" Liz whined.

"He's going with you!" Mr. Carlough sternly ordered.

Liz glanced down at the ground, frowned, and retreated. Everyone watched her sulk into the kitchen. Mr. Carlough apparently heralded Stan as a saint, and Steve remembered what Liz had said the day before at lunch: Mr. Carlough wanted Liz and Stan together because if they could combine their net worths, they'd be the most powerful family in the state. It ultimately came down to the fact that Mr. Carlough was using him. Stan finally walked into Tim's house as Mr. Carlough rushed away and sped off in his car.

Stan wore a peach-colored dress shirt underneath a pale-yellow sweater, gray slacks, and black dress shoes. His shaggy dirty-blond hair and thick-rimmed glasses remained the same. In his hand was a leather briefcase full of clothes.

"Greetings, everyone. I am glad to see my runners." Stan grinned.

9

UPON ARRIVAL

This was entirely unbelievable. Everyone in the living room was having a showdown with Stan. He was smiling back at them, pleased that he was back with the group. They couldn't get rid of him now. If they ended up leaving him behind, he'd surely tell Mr. Carlough, and no one wanted to deal with his crap.

"Gosh, who let Stan out of his cage?" Richie murmured.

Alan slowly approached Stan and held his hand out for a shake. Alan wanted to ease everything up and offer a truce with him. Stan didn't hesitate in responding to the offer.

"Stan, my man, what's up?" Alan asked.

"Nothing much. Glad to be the chaperone, if you will, on this trip. But I just wanted to know if you guys are still trying to catch this killer instead of sitting on your ugly, poor asses."

"Oh, that one for sure," Liz whispered, nodding her head. Rod held her close, comforting her after her father's outburst.

"You poor saps, invite me to your funerals." Stan chuckled.

"Shut up, will you?" Rod snapped at Stan.

"What's wrong, *Rodney*? Mad that I'm here?" Stan smirked.

"There's no reason for you to even be here, *Stanley*." Rod scowled.

"Do you even want to come with us?" Veronica asked.

"Absolutely," Stan said and grinned. "I had nothing planned for my spring break. Besides, I will make the trip more exciting. With my genius wits, you'll all survive longer than you would have without me."

The room filled with groans. Alan would've preferred that Ray Kuiper not be on his mind. They were about to leave for the lake house, where rest and relaxation awaited them. The only thing missing from this spring break was *single* girls in their bikinis. Kuiper and the whole "runners" idea were only going to be like a blot of ink on a dress shirt.

Liz glared at Stan, still very upset. It was clear that she wanted to wrap her hands around Stan's slim neck and strangle him. Tammy, in contrast, exchanged waves with Stan.

"Tim, as I was saying," Richie said, finally getting the chance to repeat the question he'd asked before Mr. Carlough's rude interruption, "can we leave now?"

"S—" Tim tried to speak.

"Yeah, let's get going," Tammy insisted before Tim could finish.

"Babe, the guys have special plans for their girls at sundown," Steve quipped.

"And none for me?" Tammy turned away, annoyed that Steve apparently had nothing of the same for her. Steve pulled her back to him.

"I didn't know you were coming until a few hours ago." Steve rested his chin on her shoulder. "But, yeah, I got a little something planned, come to think of it."

"Good." Tammy kissed Steve on the lips. He kissed her back, and she kissed him once more.

"Herpes." Liz coughed. Veronica, walking back into the room from the kitchen, laughed.

"As I was trying to say, the faster we get to the lake house, the better. All right, everyone, move out." Tim pointed to the door.

They all grabbed their stuff, and Tim showed them out. Stan stepped in front of Alan as he left, almost tripping him. *This is gonna be a blast, even if Stan's with us.* Alan had to keep his hopes high. This was his lake house. Everyone would be playing by his rules.

"All aboard, everyone," Steve announced as he stood inside the Winnebago.

The group walked up a set of stairs and into the vehicle, which featured cream walls and a new-car smell. Two beige-colored lounge chairs sat behind the driver's seat. A sink, some counters, a microwave, and a refrigerator were situated on the passenger's side of the Winnebago.

Adjacent to the microwave and fridge was a sofa with a cream-colored table directly in front of it and a two-seat couch nearby. The bathroom and shower were in the back, along with a bed obscured by a green curtain.

Richie and Tammy sat on the two-seater, while Veronica and Liz sat on the sofa with Tim. Rod took a seat on a lounge chair while Stan looked around.

"Looks like we're sitting next to each other, comrade," Stan smirked as he sat next to Rod.

From his spot at the wheel, Steve saw Stan taking a seat next to Rod. "Shit," Steve muttered to himself. But he relaxed as Rod merely shrugged, seemingly not caring about his seatmate. "Is everyone ready for takeoff?"

"Yes," everyone answered.

"Suitcases?" Alan turned around in the passenger seat, rubbing his hands together in excitement. "Check."

"Keys?" Steve poked Alan.

"Check." Alan swung a ring with two gold keys—the keys for the lake house—in front of his face.

"All right, let's go." Steve honked the horn and put the keys in the ignition, and the Winnebago started down the road.

The teenagers cheered enthusiastically as the Winnebago made its way down the street. Finally they were off to the lake house. Four long years and a ton of trust earning had passed, but now they'd finally grasped a hold of it. Nothing could go wrong.

Alan relaxed in his seat and put his arms behind his head. He crossed his legs on the dashboard. He couldn't help but act a little brazen at the moment. They were all on the way to *his* vacation house. He had to live it up at some point.

"You have directions to this place, right?" Steve asked.

"Of course." Alan pulled a map from his back pocket.

"I'm so excited! I'm so excited!" Liz bounced up and down in the backseat. Rod looked over with a smile, but Veronica emitted an irritated sigh.

"I know, right?" Steve imitated Liz's voice, rolling his eyes but keeping them on the road.

"I'm not thrilled, if that makes you guys feel any better," Rod joked, crossing his arms.

"Oh, touché," Tim agreed. "But it could be worse; I mean, we could be locked in a room with Tammy rather than having freedom."

Rod gave Tim a thumbs-up as Tammy shot grim stares at them. At Franklin Pierce High School, no one gave Tammy Heston shit. Well, not to her face like these guys were, anyway. Tammy had such influence at the school that other people were intimidated by her. Not this group, though; definitely not this group. Alan didn't buy into the crap that rich kids held power in high school. Tammy breathed loud enough for everyone to hear her.

"I feel ya, man." Rod nodded.

"You guys are so insulting!" Tammy growled. "You guys are fucking squares."

"Alan!" Rod called over, swiftly ignoring Tammy's complaining.

"Yeah, man?" Alan answered.

"How far away is this place?" Rod asked.

"It's in Petersburg. Should be four to five hours." Alan turned back, the map blocking his view of the road. "But if traffic is good, it may even be three and a half."

"Yeah, and if any of you guys brought some eight-tracks, we could listen to them soon," Steve offered.

"I brought some," Richie called to Steve.

"I'm so glad we are finally leaving," Tim stated.

"Yeah, no parents." Veronica smiled at Tim.

"No rules." Rod grinned.

"No homework," Richie added.

"And no Ray Kuiper." Liz sighed.

Tammy snickered as soon as Liz mentioned Ray Kuiper's name. "Ray Kuiper is just a legend to scare little kids." She sneered. "Clarissa and Lauren told me about him, like, a year ago, and it's pathetic how you guys are scared of a legend."

"Shut up!" Liz yelled.

"Make me, you dumb broad," Tammy shouted back.

Steve and Alan exchanged glances and shook their heads. Alan feared a fight would break out on the way. *Please—please just stop!* he hoped.

"Yeah, seriously, Tammy. Go be a bitch to Stan." Veronica laid her head on Tim's shoulder.

Stan hadn't heard Veronica; he was resting in his lounge chair.

"I don't care what you say, Leeds," Tammy replied. "There's a reason we don't allow trash on our softball team."

That jab silenced everyone. Alan's eyes widened. Veronica's face was blank, and everyone knew why. The previous school year, Veronica had tried out for the softball team but ultimately wasn't selected. The reason was that Tammy, who'd been pitching, threw a fastball directed at Veronica. It hit her in the face. Popularity apparently overruled common sense.

"No arguing!" Alan finally yelled at the girls. "I told you guys I wasn't joking, dammit."

"The odds of that are low," Richie reluctantly admitted.

The group began to calm down, and Steve stopped at a red light. Alan closed his eyes. He'd known some of this bickering was bound to happen. And it didn't take long for it to start, just as he'd expected. Alan took advantage of the newfound quiet and brought up positives. Namely, the gorgeous lake house they were on the way to.

"I hope you guys brought swimsuits. I mean, the lake isn't just for fishing," Alan remarked.

"Of course," Liz answered, bubbly.

"And if not, we could always skinny-dip," Tammy added.

The Winnebago swerved slightly, and Steve quickly got back on track. "Sorry about that, guys," he said awkwardly.

The Winnebago was choice. It rode smoothly and, when Steve turned the radio on, proved to have a radical sound system. To make matters better, all the seats were comfortable, with warm leather soft enough to make anyone fall into a deep sleep. Stan had given in to temptation already.

Tim kissed Veronica's forehead, her head still resting on his shoulder.

"Veronica," Tim whispered in her ear.

"Yeah?" She smiled.

"Are you gonna be ready for tonight?"

"I have a feeling I know what this little plan is of yours. But that doesn't mean I don't like the sound of it. Of course I'm going to be ready." She kissed him on his chin.

"Good, because I'm already ready." Tim leaned closer to her.

"I bet you are." Veronica put her head back on his shoulder and poked his thigh.

Rod had the urge to jam. He pulled out a blue rectangular cartridge from his suitcase under his seat. It was an eight-track tape of the Ramones' self-titled debut. Making sure Steve was driving carefully, Rod casually went over to the front and handed Alan the tape.

"Don't make any sharp turns; I'll beat you if you try." Rod smiled.

"I most certainly will not." Steve laughed.

As Rod got back in his seat, Alan placed the map on his lap and shoved the tape into the deck. From the opening of "Blitzkrieg Bop," the sound system really kicked in. Stan nearly fell out of his seat from the abrupt noise. He remained bug-eyed while the tape played.

Forty minutes passed. It was four fifty-five. The tape had been over for several minutes, and Richie had fallen asleep. The ride was silent except for a few horn honks, courtesy of Steve getting aggravated with slow drivers. Tim was staring out the window, disconnected from reality. He snapped out of his daze once he heard Steve's voice: "Oh shit!"

"What?" Alan asked, looking away from the map.

"Running low on gas." Steve looked back and then turned front again. "Liz, you pay for it."

Liz, who was looking in her mirror, applying foundation, frowned at Steve. "Um, no way, Steve. Make Tammy or Stan do it."

"Shut up. I'm not wasting good money on gas," Tammy sneered.

"I'm broke," Stan remarked casually.

"Tim?" Liz asked.

"Fifty bucks for booze only."

"Hurry up." Steve said as he pulled into a gas station devoid of any cars. It was a cheap one—only two pumps under the overhang. There was a beat up 7-Eleven too, and its sign was broken on the bottom right section.

"I brought forty bucks." Rod pulled the cash out of his jacket pocket.

"Here's twenty from me." Veronica leaned across and handed the money over to Rod.

"OK, I'll pay you guys back when we get home." Steve got up and retrieved the money before heading out to the pumps.

"Why did we stop?" Richie asked, waking up.

"Steve had to get gas," Tammy replied.

"Hey, what tapes did you bring?" Alan called back to Richie.

"I brought *Spirits Having Flown*."

"Good luck." Rod chuckled. "Steve's gonna hate you for that."

A couple of minutes passed. Alan skimmed through the radio stations on the FM channel. Finding nothing that appealed to his tastes, he turned the radio off and pulled a Tareyton out of the inside of his leather jacket. Alan smoked cigarettes occasionally. He had done so for the past year, usually whenever he wanted to relax. As he put the Tareyton in his mouth, Steve entered the Winnebago, took his seat, and groaned in aggravation.

"Eighty dollars is a damn rip-off." He pushed his hair from out of his face and started the engine.

"I thought it was sixty dollars," Liz said.

"Just because he got sixty dollars from his friends doesn't mean that's what the cost came out to be, you moron," Tammy scoffed.

"Oh my God, if you don't shut up, I am going to use you as gas." Alan looked back, cigarette dangling from his mouth.

"Bring it," Tammy replied, standing up from her seat.

"So, what, you're a badass now?" Liz complained. "Why don't you take your rich behind and go somewhere?"

"Agreed," Tim added.

"What the hell does this have to do with you, Tim?" Tammy questioned.

"You're just being a bitch to everyone here but Steve!" Tim shouted, pointing at his friend.

"Tim!" Steve shouted back in baffled tone.

"Quiet down!" Veronica shouted. "Stop acting like you guys are all tough."

"We are tough." Richie brashly put his chest out as if he were a hero.

"Lies," Tammy responded.

"Well, you aren't tough. You think you're badass because of your parents," Alan stated, holding on to a box of matches he'd also pulled from his jacket.

"Seriously," Richie agreed, resuming his natural state. "Hell, I think your mom was cheating, because you look nothing like your parents."

"And if so, you just got the bad genes." Liz laughed.

"And if not, well…you're as loose as your mother," Stan said. Then all was hushed.

And for the first time in a long time, Tammy didn't respond. Instead, she wiped a tear away, sat back down, and buried her face in her palms. Steve slowly rose from his seat and turned to the others. He was fuming, teeth clenched, fists tightened. He repeatedly eyed every person in the Winnebago but Tammy. The line had to be drawn.

"Guys...she's adopted," Steve confessed. "You guys are fucking assholes."

"Adopted? Why?" Stan asked.

Tammy kept quiet as Steve went over to her and kneeled down, putting his arms around her tightly to console her as best he could.

"My birth parents were murdered when I was one..." Tammy sniffled. Steve wiped a tear from her cheek.

"And they let you survive? Dammit." Richie chuckled.

Steve raised a fist at Richie, giving him an "I'm not even kidding" look. Richie quickly put his hands up and shook his head, stopping right then and there.

"And I was adopted into a rich family; otherwise I would be poor like all of you," Tammy admitted.

"Did they ever find the killer?" Tim asked.

"They didn't." She sniffled again. "But I can tell you it was around the time the strange murders began. After Ray Kuiper disappeared."

"Ray Kuiper disappeared in fifty-two."

"I know. But the killings started about a decade later, which was when I was born. It was weird because they found some evidence like fingerprints that matched Ray Kuiper's, or so they think, but it couldn't be him, because his body was found so many years before."

"So it's a mystery," Stan whispered.

"Yep," Steve responded. "So try saying shit to Tammy again, all of you, and I might end up being the killer."

Steve kissed Tammy's cheek and said a few things to her quietly. Alan could hear the words "assholes" and "anger" along with some bits about how Steve cared for her. Steve walked back to the driver's seat, and they were off.

"I'm sorry, Tammy," Tim said after a couple of minutes.

"It's fine." Tammy looked at him, no longer crying but with tearstains on her cheeks. "You guys got what you wanted—my vulnerability." She surveyed the floor.

Alan felt as though they had gone too far this time. As spiteful as she could be at times, Tammy was never *that* mean to people. Sure, she'd laugh in their faces or taunt them, but she'd never blatantly insult others' parents. Alan found himself feeling remorse for what they'd said to Tammy. It was something he'd thought he would never do. He struck a match, lit the cigarette in his mouth, and sighed.

The Winnebago zoomed along. Steve made a left and gunned down the open road, barely a car in sight. He was pissed, and it was obvious. His eyes were squinted at the road, focusing on it and it only. Alan patted his shoulder and pointed out the window.

"What? What is it?" Steve didn't bother turning to Alan.

"Over there." Alan was pointing at a black 1967 Oldsmobile convertible coming up on their right. There were four people in the car.

"What about it?" Steve asked.

"Take a closer look." Alan said, breathing out smoke.

Steve hesitantly eyed the Oldsmobile as it came into view. Alan lowered his window. Almost instantly, everyone heard the sound of disco music—more specifically, "Hot Stuff" by Donna Summer—coming from outside. Steve realized Alan was trying to annoy him.

"Fuck you, Alan." Steve groaned. "Jive turkeys and stellas. If there's anything I hate as much as hot dogs, it's this shit."

"What if you had to give them a ride?" Alan took a drag on the cigarette.

"No fucking way I'd have those cretins in a car with me. This is a drivable house, not a drivable circus. Besides, disco's dead."

Alan stifled a laugh. "KISS did disco."

"It's only a minor slump!" Steve shouted.

"Watch out!" Alan yelled abruptly.

Steve stopped short, slamming the brakes harder than he should have. Everyone in the back nearly fell over. The Oldsmobile had passed them, and no other cars were in sight.

"What's going on?" Rod asked.

"Yeah, what gives?" Steve added.

Alan, whose head was turned toward his open window and at a wild forest to his right, echoed a sigh of relief. "You almost hit something that ran across the road."

"Seriously?" Steve stepped back on the pedal.

"I don't know what it was, but we were inches away, and it was fast. You should thank me for being here to help," Alan said, blowing smoke out the window.

"Thank you?" Steve cocked an eyebrow. "You nearly got us in an accident because you wanted me to take a glance at a bunch of clowns!"

Alan merely shrugged. He flicked the cigarette outside, and Steve began driving at a normal speed again after scanning the road a few times. They hadn't hit whatever had run across the street, and everyone was all right. Nothing mattered more than that.

It took no time for Alan to fall asleep, his head drooping downward, Alan's dreams solely focused on everything bound to happen at the lake house. He hoped that the drama and tension would die down. All he had to do was manage three simple things: First, get Liz and Tammy to stop bitching at each other. Second, make sure Stan did not get on everyone's nerves. Third and most important, try his hardest to keep the group's hopes up.

The sun was going to set soon. He couldn't wait to get to the lake house and live it up. He wanted to pick up a few girls sometime during the week and bring them over. Or even invite Samantha Garfield. She always found a way back into Alan's plans. He woke up after Stan began calling his name.

"What's to come when we get there?" Stan asked.

"The world is yours when we get there, friend," Alan remarked. "It's maxed out, this lake house, and trust me—you'll find something to do."

"Sounds good," Stan replied.

The next thing everyone knew, Steve had to pull over because Stan needed to use the bathroom. He told everyone that he had a mild form of claustrophobia and that the Winnebago's bathroom was way too small for his liking. It only took a minute, and soon after, they were back on the road once more. As Steve continued down I-28, he noticed the sky changing color. "It's beautiful," he admitted.

"What?" Rod looked over.

"The sky. Rain clouds are coming in, meshing with the reds and purples from the sunset." Steve eyed the sight.

Alan glanced up from his map and nodded in approval. As Steve continued staring off into the sky, he accelerated without realizing it. The speed limit was fifty-five; Steve was going sixty-five.

Unfortunately for the teenagers, a wail of sirens came only a few moments later. Everyone groaned in astonishment. Steve hit the steering wheel as he pulled over to the side of the road.

"What the hell does the fuzz want?" Rod grumbled.

"And perfect timing too." Richie sighed. "No one has any stash on them, right?"

No one did. While the others grew irritable, Steve remained tranquil. He refused to let a cop stopping them get the best of him.

"This shouldn't take long," Steve told everyone. "We're almost there, and I'll try to give some kind of story to the cop."

A tapping noise eventually came at Steve's window. He hiccupped from the surprise and rolled the window down, forcing a smile too.

"Good evening, Officer," Steve said in a polite tone.

"Good evening. Can I see your license and registration, please?" His voice was raspy, and his breath smelled of smoke. Steve held his own breath for a quick second, and his hand impulsively reached for the window raiser.

"Um, yeah, sure." Steve turned back inside and took a deep breath of fresh air.

Steve pulled his wallet from his back pocket and handed his license to the cop. Looking it over, the cop slowly stared back at Steve with an irate expression.

"I asked for your license *and registration*." He handed the license back to Steve.

"Just a second." Steve turned back and cursed himself under his breath. He fumbled with the compartments, opening one of them. The registration was the only article he found. The officer noticed he was taking a while to retrieve his papers.

"Is there a problem, son?" The officer removed his dark sunglasses.

"No, Officer, um…" Steve became lost for words.

"Harold."

Steve nodded as he handed the registration to Officer Harold. "Yeah, you see—this isn't exactly mine."

Alan led the others in turning all eyes on Steve. Alan looked up at the ceiling, his eyes closed and fingers crossed. He hoped they weren't going to be taken into the police station. *Now that'd be a vacation…*

"So you stole it?" Officer Harold asked.

"No, that's not—"

"That is grand theft auto." Officer Harold pulled a notepad from his pocket. "I hope you understand you can serve jail time for this."

"It's my brother's camper," Steve barely managed to get in. "He's letting me borrow it for the weekend. The registration is in his name. I'm his brother, Steven Waisner."

Officer Harold looked over the registration for a couple of moments. Eyeing the paper up and down, over and over, he handed it back to Steve.

"I'm letting you off with a warning, son," Officer Harold stated. "I don't usually give out warnings, but it's because I want you all to be safe. Be careful around here. Strange occurrences have been happening around this area for the past couple of years. Vandalism, theft, arson. Be safe. Besides, I just got a call that a couple of bodies were found by a bus stop. Pretty gruesome, but I'll spare you the details. Please—be careful."

"Yes, sir. We will. And thank you." Steve nodded.

Officer Harold walked away, coughing a couple of times as Steve rolled up the window. The Winnebago started back up and went on down the road. Steve and Alan exchanged glances about what Officer Harold had told them.

The others in the back had heard it too. Liz began to shake a little bit, but Veronica was able to calm her down. Alan noticed that it was the first time she had actually done something nice to Liz. Pleased, he looked over at Rod, who just shrugged. The group couldn't have been stopped at a worse time; they were nearly at the lake house.

Steve made a left and pulled onto a dirt road. The Winnebago slowed down and followed through lush forests on both sides until it came before an immense coal-colored gate, about ten feet high, with the monogram AP on a circular plaque. A single swing set appeared directly behind it to the far left.

"AP?" Steve asked. "You don't own this house, Alan."

"My father did it; he said it's mine when I turn twenty-one." Alan grinned proudly as he unbuckled his seat belt and got up. "Hang on, guys."

Alan exited the Winnebago and rapidly unlocked the gate with one of the gold keys he had shown Steve earlier. He pushed open the gate with some force. Once the gate was fully open, the Winnebago drove forward. The sky-blue beauty of a lake house was the only thing in sight.

The lake house wasn't just a run-of-the-mill little cabin or shack; it was a massive and electrifying sight. Alan hadn't been kidding when he said this house was a looker. If only he had seen the dumbfounded expressions on everyone's faces, he'd have been amused.

Yes, his family owned all of this. It wasn't common knowledge that Alan's family was considerably well-to-do. The way Alan acted and dressed broke the stereotype of the wealthy, dapper gentleman. It was probably a big surprise to everyone that this was all his—four years from now, anyway. Alan hopped back into the vehicle, and Steve parked in a dirt parking area in front of the house.

"Holy shit!" Rod rose and ran over to the front, looking at the lake house in astonishment.

"Wait, babe!" Alan heard Liz's high-pitched voice echo throughout the camper. It all boiled down to this. The majestic lake house, a place that could possibly be what everyone needed. The getaway of a lifetime.

10

THE EXTRAVAGANZA

Veronica had never been out of Charleston her entire life. She was born there and had spent all seventeen years of her life solely in that city. If relatives wished to visit, they came over, not the other way around. Even after her parents divorced, both her mother and father stayed in Charleston so that Veronica could easily see both of them.

Even if the Leedses themselves wanted to leave town for a trip, it was barely possible. Money was tight for their family, unlike the families of most of the people with whom Veronica associated. Every member of her family worked to help with income. Veronica's job was at a local supermarket, where she was a meat-cutter trainee. She didn't mind the job, nor did she mind never leaving the town where she was born. Veronica understood from a young age that some things weren't possible now. But that didn't mean the same pertained to the future.

She hoped someday she'd go out of state—or out of the country, even. But the lake house in Petersburg was a start, even if it was only a few hours away from Charleston. It was a new experience and the start of many more, hopefully. And here at the lake house, it was time to enjoy life.

A heavy breeze hit the teenagers as most of the group jumped out of the Winnebago with their suitcases and ran toward the front door.

Veronica merely strolled behind the rest of them. She was still excited about actually being at the lake house after years of waiting, but the atmosphere seemed strange, almost gloomy and depressing. The sun setting behind the many clouds above didn't help.

As everyone gathered around, Alan unlocked the door. Years had gone by since Alan had last been at the lake house. From what Veronica knew, he honestly had no idea whether any of his family had been there in the past six years, and if so, whether anything had changed from what he last remembered.

The door opened slowly, and Alan led everyone inside. The curtains were shut, and the interior of the lake house was completely obscure; only a few rays of sunlight emerged from the gaps between the curtains. A flick of a switch by the door, courtesy of Alan, and the living room emerged from the darkness.

Wood flooring adorned the room, with a large leather couch seated in front of an elegant fireplace. A gray rug was between them. There was a staircase to the right, and a stylish bar, also wooden, was directly in the back.

"I'll just give everyone the sleeping arrangements, and you can frolic and look around for yourselves. I'm relaxing first and foremost." Alan pulled a crumpled piece of paper from his jeans pocket. "Tim and Veronica, you two have the first room on the right immediately when you get upstairs."

"Cool," Tim said. Veronica moved closer to him and locked hands with him.

"Richie," Alan continued, "you were originally going to share the room down this hallway with Steve, but now that Tammy is here, you're rooming with Stan instead."

"I see," Richie said, looking at Stan in aggravation for a second.

"Steve and Tammy are getting the room across from Tim and Veronica's. Rod and Liz, due to lack of bedrooms," Alan stated, "you guys are lucky we have a Winnebago."

Liz promptly began to pout, crossing her arms. Rod put his hands on her shoulders, trying to comfort her. Veronica rolled her eyes.

Of course Liz was about to start complaining; it was only a matter of time. Not even in the house for a minute, and Liz decided to act like a drama queen.

Spoiled brat, Veronica thought, keeping her own complaints to herself.

"Steve and Tammy should have the Winnebago! Why should Rod and I be forced to sleep out there?" Liz whined.

"Take it easy." Alan tried calming her down. "While I was at home getting ready, Rod asked if he and you could sleep in the Winnebago. I called Steve, who agreed, and that's that."

Liz asked Rod if that was true. He nodded, and Liz was forced to swallow her pride and follow Alan's directions.

"Fine," she grumbled.

As Rod took his girlfriend back outside to put their bags inside the Winnebago, Alan quickly stopped him, giving him a devious grin. "Dude," he whispered, "a couple should sleep in a Winnebago at least once." Alan nudged Rod a couple of times in the shoulder.

Rod could only smile. He patted Alan on the back and went out the door.

"Now, I have the master bedroom on the third story. Don't expect to find much up there, because that's the only thing on that floor."

"And porno magazines," Tim muttered. A couple of the others laughed.

"Don't tell everyone," Alan joked, lightheartedly shoving Tim. "Make it a great night or not, my friends; choice is yours."

Alan went down the hall and up the stairs, Tim and Veronica following. Stan and Richie went down the same hall and to their bedroom, while Steve and Tammy automatically jumped onto the couch and began making out noisily.

As Tim and Veronica parted ways with Alan, who went up the final flight of stairs, they entered their bedroom. It was spacious, and the entire room was a beige color. The couple wasted no time in tossing their suitcases by the side of the bed and quickly wrapping their arms around each other.

All alone, and everyone in the house knew better than to check in on them. They were at each other's mercy, right where they wanted to be. As Veronica's hold on her boyfriend strengthened, she began to feel uneasy all of a sudden. To add to the strange atmosphere of the lake house, she still felt a sense of distance between her and Tim.

For two years and one month, the two had been a couple, and Veronica couldn't believe her luck. Her parents had told her never to abuse the word *love*, but Veronica was more than sure she loved Tim. She knew she shouldn't have jumped to conclusions regarding him and Liz. Not trusting Tim was almost like not trusting her own parents. And even after everything that had happened after the argument, including Tim's anniversary present, Veronica still thought she wasn't doing enough to please him.

Things had been hectic between the two for the past month or so. Veronica had been working more hours than usual at the supermarket to earn more money, and they hadn't seen much of each other at all. But now the future was all that stood before them.

Now that they were at the lake house, even with its atmosphere, Veronica had some hope. *What is better than a week away from the outside world with your closest friends and a beautiful surrounding?* Veronica couldn't think of anything. And even more, she figured, her relationship with Tim would without a doubt be strengthened. As long as the tension remained low.

"Veronica," Tim began, "words can't describe how much I care about you. The past two years, and one month, have made me truly realize how strong our relationship is. And I only want it to get stronger from here on out."

Veronica knew how undeniably sappy that sounded, and it was embarrassing, to say the least. But she didn't care. She loved it when Tim was sappy. She loved it when Tim called her cheesy names like "beautiful," "lovely," and "cutie."

Her arms wrapped tightly around his neck, she smiled. "I love you so much, Tim. And nothing can go wrong on this trip."

"Yeah," Tim replied, smiling back.

His voice sounded a bit skeptical. Being a straightforward person, Veronica was not going to let that slide. She couldn't help but be somewhat concerned whenever her boyfriend sounded skeptical about something.

"I heard something in your voice, Tim," she started. "Something the matter?"

Now his face was uncertain too. Skepticism and uncertainty. Tim frowned, and Veronica put her hand on his cheek.

"It's just"—Tim sighed—"I'm just remembering what the officer told Steve a little bit ago. Vandalism, arson—"

"Tim, it's fine. The officer said *around* here, not here exactly. There's no reason to be worried."

Tim hesitated and then chose to stop overthinking everything. "Well, I guess you just know how to reassure me."

"Good." Veronica smiled somewhat seductively. "Because I only want you to be focused on one thing now. You said you had something planned for me, right?"

"Maybe." Tim slyly grinned.

Veronica removed herself from Tim's grip and lay down on the bed. She slowly lifted up her long-sleeved white midriff top, revealing only her bare chest—no bra. Picture-perfect Cs.

"*Maybe?*" Veronica bit her lower lip.

"Well, now that you put it that way…"

Tim soon found himself in the bed lying on top of Veronica, their hands intertwining as they made out. Then they found themselves almost completely naked, Tim down to his boxers and she down to a pair of light-blue panties. He smelled really good because of the Brut cologne he had on.

Tim began to kiss Veronica's neck, making her feel jittery. It never failed; she couldn't deny Tim was excellent at what he did. Of course, Tim and Veronica had had sex before, but for some reason, it felt different this time around. Not like their first time, but like the first time in a romantic setting. It felt exciting for both of them, and they also wanted more. But, to Veronica's disappointment, Tim tersely moved his body off hers.

"Shit." His voice was muffled, as his lips were still on Veronica's neck. "I left my wallet in the Winnebago, and you know what's in there. Something I need right now."

Veronica nodded. "Go and get it. Just don't take too long." She winked.

"I'd be a damn fool to leave this body waiting." Tim leaned in for another kiss before throwing his jeans back on, followed by his shirt, which he didn't button. "Be back in a sec."

"OK," Veronica teased, biting a finger gently.

I hope he doesn't leave me waiting too long…

Downstairs, Tim found Steve and Tammy still making out on the couch. They didn't notice him. Richie and Stan weren't in sight, nor were Rod and Liz. Heading out the door, Tim rushed to the Winnebago.

It was completely dark now, though porch lights and the moon above gave Tim some needed leverage. He opened the side door slightly and entered the Winnebago, going over to the table to begin searching the three-seater couch.

"Rod? Is that you?"

Tim froze. Liz's voice had come from behind the drapes. Not only did hearing her voice almost spook him out of his wits, but this was the worst place he could be now. He wanted to be back upstairs in bed with Veronica. If he didn't answer Liz, she'd get scared. If he told her it was him, she might want to talk for a bit.

"Rod?" she said again.

"It's only Tim. I'm just getting my wallet."

"Oh, Tim!" Liz shouted suddenly. "What a coincidence. I needed to talk to you about something."

"Right now?" Tim asked. He had more important things to do.

"If you wouldn't mind."

"I'm a bit busy."

"But it won't take long."

Tim wasn't going to win. If he left, Liz would start whining. Tim didn't want that. Besides, it wouldn't hurt for her to ask him something. They were friends now, able to confide in each other. Tim gave in and made his way to the green drapes, moonlight emitting from the back window.

He gently opened the drapes and peeked his head through. Liz was sitting up in the bed. She was smiling only because Tim was there. Her eyes, though, indicated fright. The covers were wrapped around her upper body, obscuring her chest. Liz pointed at the bed, wanting him to sit down.

Tim was reluctant. Rod wasn't around, and if he walked in with Tim sitting on the bed, there would be severe consequences—even if Rod merely was jumping to conclusions. Playing it safe, Tim sat on the edge of the bed.

"What is it?"

"I'll be honest, Tim. I'm kinda scared."

"Of what? Me being right here with you?"

Liz shook her head. "That's not the reason. It's about Rod."

Tim was crossing his fingers behind his back, hoping she wasn't going to tell him she's losing interest in her boyfriend. If Liz confided that she was starting to fall for him, Tim wouldn't know how to react. He took a deep breath, not wanting to move on yet curious to learn more.

"Keep going."

"You see—I love him," Liz admitted, "but I'm pondering whether or not we should, well, have sex."

Tim began to feel unnerved. He and Liz were friends, and she could tell him pretty much anything. But he didn't really want to hear about her feelings regarding sex with his good friend. Speaking of sex, Tim remembered he had somewhere important to be.

"Liz, I, uh, don't really think I should be the one you talk to about this."

"I know it's weird, but I feel like I can confide in you about things. Like, regarding you and Veronica. When did you guys figure out you were ready to sleep with each other?"

"Liz, that was a mutual decision between her and me. I can't be the one to choose when you and Rod sleep together. It's up to the both of you."

"I—I guess you're right." Liz nervously ran her fingers through her brown hair. "Decisions, decisions." She began looking down at the sheets. "I'm sorry I had to put you on the spot like that, Tim. Again, you're just the only person I can speak to here. I would've asked Veronica, if we were closer or something."

Tim quickly leaned in and hugged Liz. He had to. She sounded upset. She cared about Rod and was only trying to figure certain things out about their relationship. Tim cared about Liz's feelings; he wasn't afraid to admit that. But as he hugged her, the undeniable fear of someone walking in on them tormented his mind.

11

DANGER, DANGER

Rod finished having a can of beer with Alan and Richie in the kitchen. He tossed the can in the recycling bin underneath the sink, said good night to his friends, and left. He immediately saw Steve and Tammy on the couch together, her on top of him. It was a bit uncomfortable to watch, so Rod hastily exited the house.

The cool night air was perfect, and there was hardly a cloud in sight. Just the moon shining brightly at him. Rod watched it, thinking about the one thing that really bothered him at this point: his parents' impending divorce. It didn't take long for him to hurry over to the Winnebago's side door. Right now, all he wanted was Liz—nothing more.

Entering the camper, Rod climbed the steps and turned to his left. What he saw next rendered him speechless. Tim was leaving from behind the drapes, where Liz was. Everything came crashing down from there. Rod's expression turned into a look of horrified betrayal and anger. Tim stopped in his tracks, the shining moon above the Winnebago bringing out the glower in Rod's eyes.

Rod wasn't going to listen to what Tim had to say, even if it meant making a premature assumption. Rod didn't care. He felt that everyone was playing with his feelings, playing with his mind. He thought he'd lost everything important to him now—his home life, his girl-friend, and his longtime friend. It was time for everyone to pay. Everyone knew him as a calm and collected teenager. This was the other side of him.

"You are something else, Tim." Rod marched over to the bed-room, his finger pointed at Tim.

Tim said nothing. He merely stood where he was, not moving a muscle. Rod became even more furious because Tim wasn't owning up. Veronica apparently had been right all along.

"Wait, Rod. Listen," Tim began, only to be interrupted.

"No." Rod shook his head. "No, no, no. You listen to me. I trusted you, man. I thought you understood me. With all the things I've been going through, this is what you do to me? We were friends since kin-dergarten; we had each other's backs. Dude, I even helped you out when Tammy and all those bitches made you look like a fool in the middle of the lunchroom. Dammit, I helped you when Diane Peterson started stalking you in sophomore year. And this is the thanks I get?"

"Rod, calm down," Liz pleaded.

Rod eyes landed on her. He had promised Liz he'd never get an-gry at her, only raise his voice at people who treated her badly. But to do all that stuff and then get repaid by her *attempting to cheat on him.* Rod's eye twitched; he was enraged.

"And you," he sneered. "I thought we had something. I worked my ass off to get a date with you, to put up with all your father's shit, to deal with everyone telling me we were wrong for each other. But they were all right. It's nothing; it's all dust that's been blown away, you damn whore. You *rich* whore. I just wish I'd listened to your father."

Liz became bug-eyed. Everything about her was still, motionless, expressionless. She slowly swallowed, mouth trembling. Rod refused to become remorseful in this situation. Why the hell should he? Liz had screwed him over.

"Don't call her that!" Tim shouted.

"Shut up!" Rod shoved Tim into the wall. "I still can't believe you'd do this to me, Tim. I told you I trusted you. Trust. I can't believe I backed the two of you up when I noticed those smiles you continually give her."

Tim ran up to Rod and shoved him back. That only made Rod angrier.

"Would you just listen for once?" Tim shouted once more.

All of a sudden, Tim felt a fist smack into his face, followed by a sharp knee in the chest. Tim fell to the ground in pain, clutching his chest. He looked more anguished than Rod had expected. Martial-arts lessons in seventh grade had paid off.

"I go through hell; you decide to keep me there," Rod stated as he lifted Tim back up. He punched him again, this time in the stomach. Tim fell through the drapes and tumbled onto the bed. Liz grabbed Tim quickly, trying to keep him from receiving any more beatings.

"Rod, stop!" Liz begged.

But Rod couldn't. When one is taken for granted by people he relies on, it tends to break him from his train of rational thought. Rod's natural inclination would have been to hear the other side out. Instead, he didn't hesitate a second to grab onto Tim's leg, ripping him from Liz's grip. He then flung Tim toward the front of the Winnebago, but Tim hit the lounge chairs instead.

"Stay away; I don't want you to get hurt involving yourself in this." Rod scowled at Liz before he looked back at Tim.

Tim was motionless on the ground except for his fingers moving, trying to raise himself back up. But the pain was making it impossible. His arms were shaking, and he could barely breathe. The blows to the chest and stomach were more than he could handle.

"Pathetic," Rod scoffed.

He lifted Tim back up, but Tim struck him across the face with a vicious left hook. Rod threw Tim over his shoulder and rushed into the door, slamming Tim's back against the hard frame.

"Stay away from Liz." Rod's eyes glared. "You better believe me on this; I'll be keeping a better eye on you."

"You—fuck you," Tim groaned, on the floor in agony, trying to grasp his back.

"Don't act like you didn't see this coming," Rod said viciously.

"Listen to me, Rod!"

"You can't win everything."

"I always thought you were jealous. Jealous of everyone because we all have parents, trust in—"

Rod grabbed Tim by his neck and hit him hard enough to crack the right lens of his glasses. Tim fell against the door. "You—keep—my—family—out—of—this!" Rod shouted.

"Stop!" Liz screamed.

"Fuck you!" Tim yelled to Rod. "Maybe if you weren't such a jackass, your family would still be there, and you'd be able trust everyone around you without jumping to conclusions." All those words rolled off Tim's tongue before he could even understand what he was saying. Big mistake.

Rod grabbed Tim's neck again and began choking him. Tim could see everything flashing before his eyes, trying to blank out Rod's blank, cold expression. Rod wasn't even trying to let him go, let alone loosen his grip. That was the last thing he wanted to happen.

"Let him go!" Liz screamed. "Stop."

An idea crossed his mind, and he broke the promise he'd made to himself about releasing Tim from his grip. "Whatever," Rod sneered, letting Tim go. He took a deep breath and looked at Tim, leaning against the door for support. "You're not a friend, Tim. And I hope Ray Kuiper—or you better hope Ray Kuiper doesn't come for you. Because I won't save you—and I won't care if you're dead. I'll ask him personally to finish you off. I want you dead."

Then Rod kicked Tim hard enough in the stomach to break the door open behind him. As the door loudly banged against the side of the Winnebago, Tim flew onto the dirt below with a crashing thud. Rod watched him for a second, breathing heavily, before disappearing back inside the Winnebago.

When Tim woke up the next morning, the sun burned his eyes—or maybe it was the fact that he'd been beaten up hours earlier. He staggered up from the dirt and gravel and wiped the grime off his shirt and exposed chest. Tim felt the pain must've knocked him unconscious.

He made his way to the front of the house, not bothering to gaze inside the Winnebago. He couldn't look at Rod or Liz the same as he used to. He expected to see Veronica waiting for him inside the house, demanding to know where he had been.

It was painful for Tim to think of her at the moment. He couldn't imagine what it must've been like to have practically been stood up right when the two were about to make love. Tim grabbed the door handle, but it turned before he could move it. The door opened, and Steve appeared. He wore a plaid pajama set.

"Where the hell were you, man?" Steve asked, his voice concerned yet alarmed. "Veronica was worried sick about you."

"Uh...well—"

"Alan's making breakfast with Richie, Tammy's up, and Stan was in the shower last time I heard. Veronica's in your room brushing her hair out. Why are you out here?"

"You're probably not going to believe me."

"You don't know that unless you tell me," Steve replied.

Tim sighed. "Veronica and I were about to sleep together when I realized my wallet was inside the Winnebago, and in my wallet is a rubber. So I went out to get it, but Liz was in there."

"Oh no," Steve said.

"I'm not done. She only wanted to talk to me, and that's all—I swear. But Rod didn't believe me, and neither did his fists."

"Then what happened?" Steve asked, not really wanting to learn more, from the skeptical sound of his voice.

"I involuntarily passed out in the driveway."

"What?" Steve asked.

"She told me about her relationship with Rod, something she wanted to ask me in regard to that."

Steve cocked an eyebrow. Trying to convince his friend, Tim removed his glasses and showed Steve the crack on his lens. Tim hoped Steve would stop doubting him after seeing this. This was proof, absolute proof. Steve handed Tim his glasses back.

"I believe you, and I only hope Veronica does too." Steve frowned. "Your face does look a little wrecked. You have any other wounds?"

Shit, don't tell me I've got scrapes on my face, Tim thought. After putting his glasses on, Tim revealed a bruise on his stomach.

"Oh shit." Steve laughed. "Oh shit!"

"Shut up, you asshole." Tim jokingly hit his friend's arm.

The two shared a laugh, which looked awkward but felt satisfying. They heard Tammy's voice from inside.

"Are you guys coming?" she shouted.

"Do you know where they are?" Steve whispered.

"No idea." Tim shrugged.

"Come on!" she shouted again.

Tim and Steve nodded to each other and went back inside the house, Steve shutting the door behind him. Things seemed all good, for the most part, and Tim preferred to keep it that way for the time being.

But lo and behold, Tim was greeted with a sight he'd have rather taken care of later. Veronica was waiting on the staircase, arms crossed tightly and tapping a foot very impatiently. Initially glaring at her boyfriend, she abruptly ran downstairs and cupped his face in her hands.

"What happened to your face, Tim?" Veronica asked. "And where the hell have you been? After a couple of minutes went by, I went downstairs, and no one knew where you were. I checked outside too, to no avail. What the hell is going on?"

Total luck she didn't check the Winnebago, Tim thought, relieved. But now he had to make up a story on the fly. Steve could hear the truth because he could tolerate it more easily, and even then, he'd still shown skepticism at first. If Tim told Veronica the same thing, she'd freak out and think the worst before Tim could elaborate any further. He decided to give her an answer that was simple and to the point. If he rambled, she'd know he was lying.

"I had to rush out to a drugstore last night," he lied.

"Don't bullshit with me, Tim," Veronica said, poking him in the chest with her finger. Tim's chest was still throbbing from Rod's knee strike, and the jabbing of her nail didn't help. "The Winnebago was in front of the house when I checked outside! And why is one of your lenses cracked? Please, Tim, don't lie to me. I was worried sick about you. When I woke up this morning and saw you weren't lying next to me, I nearly called the police."

"I'm not bullshitting you, Veronica. I needed to go to the drugstore because I ended up not having any rubbers like I thought I did. The Winnebago was still there because I was inside trying to convince Rod and Liz to let me take it while they slept. Then I ended up getting into a fight with some rowdy customer."

Tim surprised himself—he didn't stutter, and it didn't come off like he was lying. He saw Steve out of the corner of his eye barely nodding, indicating he was sounding believable—to Steve, anyway.

"Why the hell you didn't go and get one from any of the other five guys here in this house is beyond me. But last night was supposed to be our night…"

Veronica turned away from Tim. Before he could respond, Alan's voice rang from inside the kitchen. "Pancakes are ready, everyone!"

Veronica spun back toward Tim and glared at him. "We resume this later." She stormed off to the kitchen. Steve patted Tim's shoulder.

"You came across as convincing, buddy. But good luck dealing with her later."

Tim frowned and left the living room, following Veronica at a distance. Tammy walked past him from the kitchen, going over to Steve and wrapping her arms around his waist. She was wearing a white nightgown and a black headband. She failed to notice Tim's wounds.

"Hey, cutie, I had fun last night." Tammy beamed.

Steve's expression quickly turned into one of lust when he heard Tammy's voice. He draped an arm around her lower waist, his hand lightly squeezing her bottom. Tammy moaned gently in return.

"I did too. Somehow, someway, I think you have some sort of power that makes me focus all my attention toward you. Whatever it is, it works." They began making out by the door as it opened.

Rod and Liz entered. Liz quickly walked past the two lovers by the door and hurried into the kitchen. Rod stopped and stared at Steve and Tammy for a second before following behind Liz. Steve and Tammy stopped making out and exchanged confused glances.

"Is he all right?" Tammy asked. "I mean, I know being in a relationship with Liz is probably like having your hand on a hot grill with a crying baby screaming in your ear, but he's never looked that way with her before."

"It's Rod," Steve responded. "You never know with him anymore, I suppose."

In the kitchen, Alan wore an apron with "Would rather be eating out than cooking" on it over a gray sweatshirt, jeans, and white Nike high-tops with blue outlining. He also had on his blue baseball cap, which was turned backward.

Richie wore a long-sleeved gray button-down, black bell-bottoms, and matching boots, a plain white apron over him. The two had spatulas in their hands and were before the stove, which had skillets of pancakes, sizzling bacon, and over easy eggs on top.

The group sat around the table, but Tim and Veronica weren't next to each other. Tim was next to Steve, an empty chair on the other side. Veronica sat between Liz and Tammy. The kitchen door opened again.

Stan strode inside and took a seat by Tim. He wore a blue dress shirt underneath a lemon-yellow sweater, gray slacks, and black sneakers. Adjusting his glasses, he greeted the others. "Good morning, everyone. Did you all sleep well?"

"I expect everyone to answer Stan's question with an affirmative." Alan grinned, setting two plates of breakfast onto the table.

Everyone responded positively, including Tim. Of course he hadn't really slept well, falling asleep by technicality on gravel instead of a bed, but if he answered negatively, he'd be questioned to no end.

"Good," Alan replied, serving some more breakfast with Richie. "Oh, and I forgot to tell you all something. It's rather important. When it comes to food, please eat inside the kitchen. Do not eat on the couch. Three-thousand-dollar leather."

"Three-thousand-dollar leather, my ass." Richie laughed, sitting across from Stan and placing a sizable bottle of syrup in the middle of the table.

"Oh, but it is." Alan took his seat between Richie and Rod.

"More pancakes?" Steve looked at his plate. "Seems like your specialty."

"You could say that." Alan chuckled as Tim passed the syrup to him. "I also know how to whip up some mean waffles, but there's not a waffle iron here."

When Alan thanked Tim for the syrup, he saw the cracked lens on his glasses. He tapped Richie. They didn't say anything initially. But then Alan and Richie saw Tim's bruises.

"Tim, what happened to your glasses?" Richie asked.

The entire group stared at Tim, saying nothing and anticipating his answer. Tim replied without hesitation.

"It's nothing, Richie," he answered, leaving it at that.

It didn't take them long to finish breakfast and do things among themselves until Alan and Richie had finished doing the dishes. Once they were done, everyone would be able to plan out what they were going to do for the day.

Tim was lying on the couch, an ice pack on his stomach for the bruise. He also inspected his face in the upstairs bathroom to see how badly Rod had messed it up. Fortunately it could've been way worse. Only a small scuff on his lower right cheek—probably from his crash to the gravel. The bruise on his stomach was the only mark Rod had caused. Sitting next to him was Stan, reading *The Art of Computer Programming, Volume 1,* by Donald Knuth. Veronica was next to Stan, watching the television and ignoring Tim's presence. Steve and Tammy were flirting by the bar in the back, while Rod and Liz were nowhere to be found. Soon, Veronica got up from the couch, and Tim took notice.

"Where are you going?" Tim asked her.

"Why does it matter?" she scoffed, heading for the stairs.

Tim removed the ice pack and followed, catching up to her at the bottom of the staircase.

"Come on, Veronica. I'm sorry it seemed like I ditched you last night. I didn't mean to take such a long time at the drugstore, and I should've told you I had to run out."

"Yes," Veronica replied coldly as she continued up the stairs. "You should've."

Ever a determined boyfriend, Tim kept following Veronica. He wasn't just going to put this aside. Veronica was furious with him, and he had to convince her that he was truly sorry. Whatever it took—he wasn't going to back down this easily.

"Veronica, I don't know what else to say aside from my apology. There's nothing else I can do about my actions last night. I was wrong to ditch you; I know that."

The two entered their bedroom, and Veronica sat on the bed. She glanced up at her boyfriend. Veronica still was probably upset with him, and Tim wished she, at the very least, could see he wanted to make up for what he'd done. She motioned for him to come closer to her. As he did, Veronica held on to his hands.

"OK. I forgive you, Tim," she explained. "But I just don't want something like this to happen again. You know I don't forgive easily, but for you, I can...for certain things, that is. You're my boyfriend, and I should take into consideration what you're telling me. But do you promise this is the truth?"

"I promise." Tim hated having to lie like that, but telling Veronica the actual truth would lead to more pain than the beating he'd received. "And nothing like this will happen again." Tim smiled as Veronica leaned in and hugged him firmly.

Veronica let go of him and went over to the bathroom door.

"You gonna shower?" Tim asked.

"You gonna join me?" Veronica teased.

Tim had an answer on the tip of his tongue, but Veronica rushed over and grabbed his hands. She led him into the bathroom, turned the shower on, and quickly removed her clothes. Tim couldn't help but leer. What could he say? Nothing. And he didn't want to either. Tim stripped out of his clothes and entered the shower right behind Veronica, watching the water caress her skin.

Tim was no longer a child having to abide by his parents' rules. There was nothing that could have been better than this moment. Nothing—not Rod, not Liz, not Ray Kuiper—could ruin it. This was one of those rare moments that only came by once in a lifetime, and Tim would be damned if he let it go. And from that moment on, all Tim could see was steam. All he could feel was Veronica.

An hour of surreal passion had passed. For the first time in a long time, Tim understood the meaning of rest and relaxation. He had on a yellow Devo T-shirt, dark-blue bell-bottoms, and his Italian leather boots.

Tim left his bedroom and moved on downstairs, jumping onto the couch and lying there for ten minutes. No one was else was in sight. Veronica was in the bathroom doing her hair, without a doubt feeling the same as her boyfriend—or so he hoped.

Tim took the time to bask in his glory, remaining on the couch until the door opened and everyone else came inside. Veronica made her way downstairs at the same time. Tim gazed up.

"What were you guys doing out there?" Tim inquired.

"Richie was just showing us some Ray Kuiper memorabilia that he brought in the Winnebago," Alan answered.

"Speaking of which," Richie said, "I found this in here." He handed Tim a black wallet. "You must've forgot it in your seat yesterday."

Tim, who had rolled his eyes at the mention of Ray Kuiper's name—*they're still on this topic?*—nevertheless thanked Richie and put the wallet in his back pocket.

"What kind of Kuiper stuff did you bring, Richie?" Veronica asked.

"Random clippings from the sixties that mentioned him. I found them at the library by my house and checked them out," Richie said.

"Do any of you think he's going to appear anytime soon?" Rod joked.

"Oh, definitely," Stan responded, also jokingly. "What better time than now to train my runners?"

Though everyone groaned when they heard Stan mention the idea of runners, they weren't as harsh as they usually were. Tim wondered if the others had gotten to know Stan when he was busy last night with Rod.

"You all want something to drink?" Alan asked. "I brought a cooler along with me, and it's in the kitchen now. Besides, now that we're all dressed, we can think of something to do."

Everyone nodded, and Alan went inside the kitchen to retrieve the cooler. The group sat around the couch, with Steve and Richie lightheartedly taking a seat on Tim's legs, which were resting on the couch, causing Tim to try to push them off him. Alan appeared moments later, tugging a red cooler through the door.

"Might have to swing over to the supermarket later," Alan said. "Didn't bring as much food as I should've. Oh well, at least we got brews."

While people began sauntering to the cooler, Tim lifted himself up, Steve and Richie now off his legs.

"So, what did these articles go over about Ray Kuiper, Richie?" Tim asked.

"Pretty much the same thing," Richie replied, helping Alan open the cooler. "Sightings of him around Charleston, and even one that was printed on the ten-year anniversary of his disappearance. Interesting stuff, I have to admit."

Alan and Richie opened the cooler, and the entire group reached in for drinks. But as luck would have it, Tim, who'd pulled a drink out quickly, felt the back of his hand accidentally hit something as he brought the can toward him. Everyone noticed Stan reaching for his nose, some blood trickling down his fingers.

"What the hell, Tim?" Alan yelled in astonishment. "It's just beer!"

Liz rushed over to the kitchen to get the ice pack back from the freezer, as she was the one who'd put it away after Tim followed Veronica.

"I—I don't know what just happened," Tim stammered. "It was an accident, though."

"You know what…" Alan sighed. "Tim, I think it's best we leave you alone here for a couple of hours." His voice was firm as he grabbed the ice pack and some paper towels from Liz and handed them to Stan, who pressed it all against his nose. "You start trouble at a drug-store, you look like you got beat up a bit, and now this. It's too much to handle right now." Alan took his cap off momentarily.

And if things couldn't possibly have gotten any worse…

"What the fuck?" Veronica screamed upon realizing what had exactly happened after the initial confusion. She gave her boyfriend a harder time than Alan had. "What is going with you, Tim? Why are you starting these fights? Why have you been acting like a total jack-ass to the others lately?"

"Me? What the hell has gotten into *everyone* recently?" Tim shouted back. "I'm sorry. It was a damn accident."

"Chill out," Steve whispered.

"No way." Tim pushed him away, but Steve responded by pinning him down to the floor to cool him off. The hardwood hit Tim's head.

"Hey, stop!" Liz screamed, quieting the room. "This is all uncalled-for. No one needs to be fighting anyone."

"She's right." Stan held his nose as it continued to bleed. "It seems like everyone here has been through a lot this past week—and especially these last few days. Let's get our mind off things, go swimming."

"I agree," Veronica responded. "We all need a break from Tim. Let's leave."

"You can't mean that, Veronica?" Tim got up from the floor.

"Maybe this'll show you I do." Veronica slapped Tim hard across his face.

A shocked Tim stared at his girlfriend—with whom he had just spent such a great time—bewildered. One act, an accident, and she turned against him like that. His reddened cheek burned from the slap.

"You're leaving me here alone? But the lake is just outside the house!" Tim shouted.

"It's so you can calm down," Alan said, sounding a hell of a lot more concerned about his well-being than Veronica.

Tim was the major enemy in the house once more. He sighed, no longer wishing to argue. "It's fine, really. I guess I need this…"

Alan put his hand on Tim's shoulder. Tim noticed his friend's disappointment in having to go along with this. Alan was only doing it for Tim's benefit, not because he hated him. Alan returned to the others. "The lake is just out back. Let's get going."

"I'm staying here," Steve stated. This caught quick attention.

"How come?" Richie asked.

"I think you guys are all making a big deal about nothing; that's why." Steve sat down on the couch.

"Well…all right," Alan quipped.

Tammy elected to stay back too, for Steve's sake. The rest of the crew got into their bathing suits and went out the door, Stan still holding an ice pack to his nose and Richie dragging the cooler behind them.

Tim watched Veronica go out the door last, the way her purple bikini looked on her body. She turned his way, shook her head in anger, and slammed the door behind her. Tim slouched on the couch, cracking open a beer.

"What are you two gonna do to pass the time?" Tim asked, even though he didn't really care about the question or their answer.

"You already know." Steve grinned as Tammy began kissing his cheeks.

"Have fun. Don't be too loud." Tim grimaced.

As Steve and Tammy went into the kitchen, Tim downed half of his beer and set the can on the wood floor below. He hadn't had a beer since six months ago, at Alan's birthday party. Before Tim knew it, he was fast asleep.

12

WHATEVER HAPPENS...HAPPENS

Tammy and Steve, on the other hand, were on the dining table, making out aggressively. There was something about Steve that brought out this animalistic side of Tammy, and she had no regrets. It felt good; she liked it. And it satisfied Steve.

"We can't do this in here," Steve teased.

"Why not?" Tammy bit his bottom lip gently.

"Tim's in the living room. Why not go back to the bedroom?"

"You're gonna have to do something to provoke me to catch you so I can bring you down onto a bed." Tammy gave him a sultry leer.

"Easy." Steve pulled her headband off and rushed out of the kitchen.

"Steve! Don't think you can hide from me!"

When Tammy jumped off the table and charged out of the kitchen, Steve wasn't in sight. The only person she saw was Tim, who was sleeping on the couch. Seeing him without anyone else around made her think about when she'd laughed in his face all those years ago. She moved on, resuming her search for Steve to try to block the image from her mind.

Tammy knew she could be a bitch, but sometimes she wondered whether that was going to help her get through life. *Upstairs or outside?* she thought. Tammy decided to venture outside. If Steve had hidden upstairs, he was surely not taking the game seriously. She knew the longer he evaded capture, the more enthusiastic she would be to bring him down. That wasn't to say she didn't want to already.

Tammy stood on the porch and searched around. Steve had to be hiding. Tammy didn't want this to take too long, however. The more she searched—in bushes, behind the house—the more she thought about Steve, his body, and the way he was in bed. He wasn't her first time, and neither was she his. Thing was—Steve was her best.

Funny, they both had reputations around the school. There was one difference. She was a girl, so sleeping around made her a slut. But because Steve was a guy, everyone—the guys and the girls—thought he was a stud. No one would expect that from Steve; he didn't look the part. He was slim, not even muscular—though he still had abs on his trim frame.

Tammy knew from school gossip that Steve was unable to hold relationships. His relationships with his first four girlfriends each had lasted between three weeks and five months. The reasons for those breakups were that the first girl was into hard drugs, the second had to keep him a secret from her parents and it just wasn't working, the third was a rebound, and the fourth ended up treating Steve more like a friend than a boyfriend.

And in between all the breakups, Steve had flings with other girls. Steve wasn't a person who took things for granted, like Tammy admitted she did. She was also one of the very few people who had heard the real reason Steve's relationship with Dawn Martinez had fallen apart.

It was the only gossip that never spread around the school, because the girls liked Dawn and refused to start stuff behind her back. The truth was that Steve unknowingly got Dawn pregnant. The next thing you know, she and her family moved out of Charleston. She broke up with Steve by placing a simple note on his locker on her last day, which was the reason why he got sullen whenever her name was brought up. This even happened if someone simply used a phrase like "up at the crack of dawn." No one knew what happened with Dawn and the baby.

So Steve got treated like the big man on campus while Tammy, who was like Steve, was forced to cope with everyone thinking of her as a slut. Tammy admitted she slept around but never when she was in a relationship. Tammy was just hardly ever in relationships; when she was, it was a week of nothing.

All the constant thinking about relationships made Tammy wonder whether Steve was only a fling. While she thought they loved each other—though she comprehended that may have been a bit premature—they had never officially called each other boyfriend or girlfriend. Even Steve's friends thought of her as his newest fling.

And that's what Tammy's goal was. She decided that when she found Steve, she'd get him to reveal his true feelings first—to see if he wanted to be in relationship with her, like she wanted to be with him. The only place Tammy hadn't searched was the Winnebago, and she quickly entered it.

"Steve?" she asked. No answer.

Tammy looked back outside, just in case Steve had in fact been hiding somewhere out there, waiting to make his return to the house while she was in the camper. But there was no sign of him. Tammy frowned.

She explored the Winnebago again, inspecting this time underneath the table near the three-seater couch. She bypassed the bathroom door, as it was slightly ajar. *Steve's not that bad of a hider,* she thought to herself. Instead, she swiped open the green drapes leading to the bed. He wasn't on it or under it. Tammy shook her head. She figured he must've been inside the entire time while she was outside searching high and low for him. She felt silly, but she nevertheless smiled and began to make her way out of the Winnebago. And then the bathroom door opened.

"Oh, you've got to be kidding me, Steve." Tammy laughed. "I can't believe you tricked me!"

But the person who exited the bathroom wasn't Steve. The figure raised a wrench over Tammy's head. She had no time to react, no time to scream or run. It all happened too fast. The wrench came crashing down on the top of her head, hard enough to embed itself deep into her skull. Almost instantly, she blacked out and her body fell to floor, blood flowing down her forehead. The assailant kneeled by her immobile body and tore the wrench from her skull, causing even more blood to pour from the wound. One more smash of the wrench to her head sprayed blood all over the attacker's clothes and face. The blood drained onto the floor of the Winnebago, drenching Tammy's face.

"Take care," the killer said.

13

SHE'S NOT THERE

The sound of the others coming through the front door woke Tim. He didn't budge from the couch. Serenity no more, as the others probably still thought the same of him as they had when they left. On the bright side, his darkly tinted glasses obscured his eyes. He gazed over and heard them all talking and having a good time—every single person.

Even Stan, who'd gotten only a bit of a bloody nose from being hit in the face *by accident*, mingled well with the others. And Rod and Liz were sharing smiles and laughs as well. *I guess I am the person who causes the tension around here*, Tim painfully admitted to himself. He would've frowned, but the others might've guessed he was awake. Alan and Richie approached Tim, Richie shaking Tim's leg.

"We're back, man," Richie said.

"I see," Tim answered in an intentionally monotonous voice.

The two friends still weren't happy about leaving Tim inside, but Tim really couldn't care less by this point. He was angry with himself mainly, even if he was more relaxed at this point. It couldn't have been that bad.

"How are you feeling?" Alan asked.

"Peaceful," Tim said.

Tim got up from the couch and went past the others, going upstairs. He wasn't in the mood for small talk with them. Alan and Richie understood Tim had every right to be annoyed with them both.

Upon getting to the top step, Tim glanced back down momentarily. He saw Veronica, who gave him the same stare of despair. She sighed, and Tim walked away. He looked over toward Steve's room. The door was open, and Steve was asleep, clutching a black headband in his hands. He noticed Tammy wasn't in there; he assumed she was in the bathroom. Tim proceeded into his room and closed the door.

The group downstairs continued to socialize. They were still somewhat wet, as they'd gone back in before the towels could dry them completely. Veronica removed her towel and tossed it on the couch, causing Alan to remind her how much the leather couch cost. She retrieved the towel and threw it over her shoulder.

"We have to plan more stuff like this, guys. Imagine all the things we can do this week." Rod smiled to himself.

"Tell me about it." Richie grinned. "I mean, my gosh, Alan, you have to let us know more about this place."

"Easy, easy, comrades." Alan flicked up his baseball cap, which was wet as well. "There's something just a short drive from here. A mysterious building that was started but never completed. It's called Private Property X."

"Private Property X?" Liz asked, sitting on the couch with Veronica. "Is this Private Property V?" she asked, pointing to Veronica, who slapped her forehead at the comment.

"No, Liz." Alan contained his laughter. "First of all, the X stands for 'ten.' Secondly, Private Property X was going to be owned by my uncle. However, he was killed in a freak electrocution accident on the grounds. It's a nice place, though. Smaller than this lake house, but that's the way it should be. Private Property X was supposed to be more of a family home. But since my uncle died, plans were scrapped, and all that's there is a building with nothing inside. Rather creepy."

"Then let's go at night," Stan offered.

"No way!" Liz cried. "Once it hits nightfall, I'm going to sleep. After the past few days, the darkness scares me."

"You've got to be kidding." Veronica said.

Footsteps came rushing down the stairs. Steve appeared, his face betraying worry.

"Hey, Steve, what have you been up to?" Richie asked.

"Just woke up from a nap," Steve quickly replied. His words were rushed and nervous. "Have you guys seen Tammy?"

"She stayed here with you and Tim," Veronica explained.

"I know that, Veronica. But after you all left, she wanted to play a game that involved her chasing after me. I went upstairs, and I think she may have gone outside to look first. But I ended up passing out because I hardly got any sleep last night."

No one knew where Tammy was. Steve became even more worried. The others had been at the lake for two or three hours. Veronica hadn't seen her at all, not even in the wooded area around the lake. If she hadn't gone to the lake, then where could she have gone?

It wasn't like Tammy to disappear like that. She always wanted people to know where she was or where she was going. Steve fretted, pacing back and forth at the bar to think, but Liz calmed him.

"Come to think of it, Steve, I came inside to get towels when you must've been napping. I saw Tim napping too. As I went back out, I saw someone going through some bushes to the left of the house. I was frightened until I noticed the person had long hair," Liz said.

"Had to have been Tammy," Alan chimed in. "She must've seen you were asleep and went on through those bushes because there's a path there leading around the lake."

It was plausible. Steve nodded and stopped pacing. He just hoped she'd be back shortly. It was going to be getting dark soon. To make him feel better, Veronica reminded Steve that Tammy knew where she was in case it was getting too late. As for why she wanted to take a walk alone, Steve could only think that maybe she just wanted to spend some time with herself.

Steve's worrying about Tammy brought out the same feeling in Veronica regarding Tim. She excused herself from the others, went upstairs, and stood in the hallway to throw on a spare set of clothes she had taken outside with her. It was only a gray T-shirt, dark jeans, and sandals. Shaking out her wild black hair, Veronica knocked on the door to the room.

"Yes?" Tim's voice expressed aggravation from behind the door.

"Tim, it's me. Can I come in?"

There wasn't an answer. Instead, the door swung open, and Veronica saw Tim make his way to a dresser across the room. He was putting his clothes away from the suitcase.

"What do you want?" Tim sighed.

Veronica moved inside and closed the door behind her. She went up to Tim, who didn't bother making eye contact with her.

"I just want to know how you're feeling. I saw how quickly you left after Alan and Richie said hi to you." Veronica sat down on the bed.

"I'm fine."

"Giving me these small answers tells me otherwise," Veronica stated. Tim glanced at her briefly before turning back to the shirts he was putting away. "You have every right to be upset, and I understand that."

"Do you?" Tim asked, going back to the bed to put away some socks. "Because it seems as though you treat me like everyone else does. You never let me explain my side of the story; you jump right to conclusions. You did it at Liz's house, thinking that because we were smiling at each other, we were probably fooling around behind your back. And you don't think you did, but you damn well pulled the same stuff when I accidently hit Stan in the face. Slapping me didn't help any."

"Maybe I was just overreacting, Tim, and I didn't mean to. It's just been a problematic few days—that's all."

Tim finally kept his eyes on Veronica for more than a few seconds. He placed the socks in the drawer and rested against it, crossing his arms. "And I'm the problem, aren't I? I saw how happy you all were when you came back. A few hours away from Tim, and everything is back to normal. Is that it?"

"I never said that, and I don't mean that," Veronica argued.

"But you agreed to it!" Tim snapped. "When Alan suggested you all should get out of here, you didn't protest it. No, you just went along with him and everyone else."

"I didn't know what to think." Veronica shrugged.

Tim didn't answer her this time. Instead, he went back to the suitcase and proceeded to remove his jeans and bell-bottoms. Veronica sighed and turned around to gain her composure. When she felt like she had, she spun back around toward Tim. "Just because I agreed with Alan on that does not mean I don't care for you, Tim. I only felt like we needed to relax. If you were by yourself, you could calm yourself down."

Tim placed a pair of jeans and a pair of bell-bottoms in the drawer and headed for the door. He was tired of listening to her. "Whatever."

Veronica got off the bed and grabbed Tim before he could reach the threshold. She was close to pleading with him at this point. Not once had Veronica thought their relationship would fall to this all-time low. What made it worse was how long they'd known each other, since kindergarten, and how close they grew until their relationship commenced in high school. The feeling made her sick, and it only was getting worse. And she felt Tim moving farther and farther away from her, both physically and mentally.

"Tim, I'm sorry I didn't support you. And I'm sorry I slapped you. I wasn't thinking of the best for you when I should've been. Please just understand that."

Veronica was close to tearing up as she buried her face in Tim's chest. She held Tim close to her, but he didn't reciprocate by hugging her. He remained still, just standing motionless as Veronica clutched him. As angry as she knew he was with her, Veronica was content enough

Tim didn't just walk away. That would have been like rejecting her. And Veronica still loved Tim. Before long, he put his arms around her.

ॐ

Downstairs, Richie and Alan were watching television with Stan. Steve sat at the bar, staring out at the patio and waiting for Tammy to return as the sun continued to set. Rod and Liz were on the patio themselves, watching the sunset together.

Conflicting emotions ran out of control throughout the house, but people like Richie remained optimistic. It was hard to do so, considering every time the group was together lately someone ended up fighting. Richie could only wonder why. What could've started this downward spiral in how everyone reacted with one another?

The legend of Ray Kuiper? The sleepover in the school? The strange writings in the woods? Meeting Stan? What the hell was it? Richie could cross off the last one. Stan had to have been pulling an act the entire time when they first met him. The guy was harmless. He was sitting with them and watching *World News Tonight* on ABC like it was *Monday Night Football*. Still, what was going on with them? But Richie had an idea. The one thing that could ease everyone's mind: marijuana.

"Alan, my man, I think I know exactly what could calm us all down at this point," Richie said.

"And that would be?" Alan pushed his baseball cap from over his eyes.

"I happened to bring a bit of hash with me in my bag."

"You jackass." Alan hit his friend's shoulder lightheartedly. "I thought you said you didn't have any when we got stopped by that cop."

"I knew we weren't all going to be interrogated." Richie laughed. "Please, Alan, I know what I'm doing."

"Why you didn't tell us this earlier is beyond me."

"I wanted to save it for a special occasion, like the gang chugging beers and putting some music on. Anyway, want me to get it?"

"I'd be an idiot to decline." Alan chuckled.

Richie got up from the couch and tapped Stan on his shoulder. "Have you ever smoked before?"

Stan shook his head. "My parents would tar and feather me if they found out. But it never hurts to try, right?"

That remark almost knocked Richie off his feet. He and Alan grinned, with Alan patting Stan on the back in immense approval. That proved it. Stan Alewine was chiller than they'd both imagined.

"Good stuff!" Alan grinned.

Richie was heading for his room when he noticed Steve. He was tempted to ask Steve if he wanted to join them. It would be a way for him to get his mind off Tammy's being gone for the time being. But Richie decided against it and proceeded to his room. Rod and Liz returned from the patio.

"See Tammy anywhere?" Steve asked hopefully.

The two shook their heads. Tim came downstairs by himself and went over to the others. Before he could say anything to Veronica up in the room, she'd ended up falling asleep holding on to him. Tim had laid her on the bed and covered her up before leaving the room. Maybe a nap would make her feel better.

Tim asked Steve where Tammy was. Steve told him she was out taking a walk but had been gone for hours. Rod walked into the kitchen to move some of the beers and other assorted drinks from the cooler to the refrigerator as Tim felt a poke on his shoulder. He turned around.

"Hey, Tim." Liz smiled. "How have you been? You feel any better?"

Tim looked at Steve and saw his friend's sudden change of face.

"Should I?" he whispered.

"I'll be honest—I'm skeptical." Steve frowned.

"About what?" a voice spoke up.

Tim saw Rod appear behind Steve. It was out of the blue, a complete surprise, as he'd just gone into the kitchen.

"It's nothing," Tim said.

"Oh." Rod nodded. "I see."

Liz shrugged as Rod put an arm around her. She waved, and the two sat down on the couch next to Stan with no problem.

"He sure trains her well," Steve sneered.

"Are you still having problems with Liz?" Tim asked.

Steve nodded. "I just don't like the way she and Tammy interact. And Liz generally annoys the hell out of me. I don't hate her, but she can be unlikable at times."

"She really isn't all that bad," Tim admitted.

And though he didn't state it—merely out of respect for his friend and not to offend him—Tim could honestly say the same thing Steve said regarding Liz about Tammy too.

14

THE CLOCK TICKS

It was 8:21 p.m. Alan was cooking two frozen pizzas he'd had buried at the bottom of the cooler. Someone had to go out to the supermarket by tonight or tomorrow, as Alan had only brought so much food. Steve was the only other person in the kitchen, his face buried in open palms. He was worried sick at this point. Tammy was still gone, and he couldn't stop thinking about it.

Who could blame him? Alan would've reacted the same way if Samantha Garfield suddenly went missing for hours and there was no way to reach her. The people you care a whole lot about mean more than you think. That was fact. Alan opened the oven door and sprinkled some crushed red pepper onto both pizzas.

"Alan, do we have any flashlights around here?" Steve asked.

"There's one in my bag. Why?" Alan remained focused on the pizzas as he slammed the oven shut.

"I have to go out and find Tammy."

Alan looked up at the old-fashioned clock over the window, which would have provided a clear view of the lake if it weren't dark out. He too was aware Tammy should've been back already, considering a walk around the lake wouldn't have taken this long.

"All right, but be careful. Are you going to take anyone with you?"

Steve shook his head. "I got this, Alan. I'll be back."

As Steve left the kitchen, Alan remembered that Richie had never come out of his bedroom. But Alan had an idea of what might've happened there. Richie, upon smelling the weed, immediately began smoking it and was likely in a haze. His best friend could be a bozo at times, and that's one of the reasons Alan was so close to him.

Alan wasn't the kind of person who worried easily; he felt it did more harm than good in the long run, especially if there ended up being nothing to worry about. Alan had adopted this thought process when he was younger—namely, during the freshman-year party he had thrown.

When Alan had planned the party, he wasn't worried. When more people showed up than expected, he wasn't worried. When his parents came home earlier than expected…he worried. OK, there were some exceptions to his philosophy, but everyone has a limit.

If Alan were Steve, he would've gone out looking for Tammy earlier instead of just sitting around and waiting for her to come back. Then again, he also would've made sure she hadn't wandered off alone in the first place. But this was his property, his grounds. It was secure, and there was nothing going on around here. He was sure.

Alan knew this place like the back of his hand, even if it had been years since he'd last been at the lake house. Nothing had changed, with the exception of his initials monogrammed on the front of the gate (of which he was absolutely proud). Once he turned twenty-one, the lake house was all his.

Alan loved this place. He could see himself coming here as a retreat in the future, preferably with Samantha Garfield. If they hadn't constantly broken up for the stupidest reasons, they would've been together longer than Tim and Veronica, with just about three years under their belts. Sam was the girl he was always running back to.

He couldn't even remember how many times they'd broken up and gotten back together, but they were still soul mates, in his eyes. If a beautiful girl gave him her number, he'd still take it. But it was only a cover to make the others think he was over Samantha. With friends like Richie and Rod, he felt it would be wimpy to constantly yearn after a girl who couldn't keep a relationship with him. Alan hated having to cover for himself, and when they got back to Charleston, Alan was going to call Samantha and tell her he didn't want to lose her anymore.

Fucking relationship chatter, Alan thought. *Why is this topic always on just about every teenager's mind?* The smell of the pizzas in the oven snapped Alan back to reality. Wearing his "Would rather be eating out than cooking" apron, Alan put oven mitts on and pulled the pans out, placing them on the counter.

"Pizza's ready!" Alan called to the others.

It took no time for Tim, Rod, Liz, and Stan to come in the kitchen and take their seats around the table. It seemed so much larger than it had this morning; there had been more people then. Alan cocked an eyebrow.

"Where's Veronica?" he asked.

"She's napping," Tim answered. "Speaking of which, where's Steve going? I tried asking him, but he rushed out the door before I could say a word."

"He's going to look for Tammy. You all have to admit it's a bit strange she hasn't come back yet." Alan retrieved a pizza cutter from one of the drawers.

Not one of them disagreed. Surely Tammy should've been back before sunset. Tammy didn't seem like the kind of person who would be all right with staying outside in the dark in an area she had never been before.

"And where's Richie?" Stan asked.

"He's probably in a marijuana-induced haze right now." Alan laughed.

"Since when the hell did we have dope here?" Tim exclaimed.

"I had no idea until he told me," Alan admitted, grabbing four slices of pizza and placing two on a plate, which he served to Rod.

The dinner plates had been set before those in the kitchen. It didn't take long for a conversation to emerge that centered on what was on everyone's mind.

"Alan, how long is a walk around the lake?" Liz asked.

"Only twenty-five minutes, at most."

"Jeez." Tim took a bite of his pizza—pepperoni and sausage. "Is it bad that I'm starting to become a bit concerned as well?"

"Not at all," Alan responded. "I am…a bit."

"Same," Stan added.

"You guys are too glum." Liz sighed. "You should think like me about this situation—positively."

Only Rod didn't pitch in. He continued to eat his pizza, keeping to himself. However, he did nod in accord with his girlfriend. Alan could understand if he wasn't too worried. People expressed the feeling of worry in different ways—some not at all. It was completely possible Rod was only trying to stay calm.

Alan expected Steve to be back any minute and to hear Tammy saying anything that ranged from "It's beautiful out there" to "It's so creepy out there" to "Why the hell did you leave me out there?"

Getting up from his seat, Alan removed a beer from the refrigerator. He cracked it open and downed half of the can in a couple of seconds. It was no surprise that Alan was trying to keep cool about Tammy's being out late. He was doing a rather good job at it so far.

How else was he supposed to react? Losing his relaxed manner would only make the others do the same. Even though his stomach began to do flip-flops from worrying, Alan refused to express anything but composure.

"Excuse me, guys." Stan stood up from the table.

"Where are you going, Stan?" Alan asked.

"Bathroom," Stan answered.

Alan nodded, and Stan walked out of the kitchen.

Stan went down the hallway, past the living room, to his and Richie's bedroom. The door was closed and locked, so Stan knocked on it just in case Richie was sleeping. "Richie?" he asked.

There wasn't a response. Stan didn't feel like waking him up. Plus, the bathrooms in the bedrooms weren't exactly the largest, and Stan felt a bit uncomfortable in them.

Shivering from the thought of going to one of the smaller bathrooms, he walked back out of the hallway. He briefly considered using one of the bathrooms upstairs but assumed they were small too. Stan shivered again and instead left through the front door, deciding to do his business outside.

Stan hated his claustrophobia. The bathrooms in the house weren't even that small—thankfully nothing like the one in the Winnebago. Now, *that* one was scary. Stan's claustrophobia had caused him to panic in the slightest of situations. On the best of days, his worst enemy was the size of the Winnebago bathroom. On the worst, a subcompact's backseat was all it took.

Stan hated being in standard cars at all, preferring to be driven in his family's limousine. Of course, this stance made people think Stan was one of those wealthy snobs. Wealthy he was, but Stan was the furthest thing from a snob. He liked the peace and quiet, and the two days he had spent with the group were the noisiest he had been through in years. He actually didn't mind, though; the change was interesting. Stan enjoyed learning new things, and this was a new experience.

He admitted to himself that he could've shown his true self to the group when he had met them the day before, but he'd wanted to know their strengths and weaknesses, just as a test. That was the reason Stan was often perceived as something of a creeper.

He'd wanted to frighten them, see what their reactions would be. It ended up backfiring at first, of course, but as his regular self now, he felt like he'd got in just fine. At the lake, he was able to get the likes of Liz and Rod to laugh at his jokes. He'd always thought Liz hated him—Rod too, considering her father preferred Stan and wasn't afraid to show it.

But Stan's crush on Liz had faded long ago. He knew she wasn't into him, and he understood it. He couldn't deny that Liz was an attractive girl. She simply wasn't right for him. Truth be told, Stan despised being Mr. Carlough's right-hand man. He knew Liz's father wanted them together for additional wealth; Stan was far from stupid. He only went along with it to make his own father happy. Still, Stan liked to occasionally hit on Liz to irritate her.

Stan held high hopes for what was to come at the lake house. He had a couple of friends at school, but they were all alike, interested in similar topics. Everyone on this trip was different in one way or another. Quite possibly, with the way things were slowly turning around, he could make some of them his new friends.

Alan and Richie had no problem with him, and neither did Steve or Veronica. Stan also knew that what Tim had done to him earlier was an accident. Why would Tim have wanted to hit him out of nowhere? Stan didn't understand the ordeal, and he also felt bad about being the cause of what eventually ensued with Tim and the others. All Stan could hope for was some type of reconciliation for the entire group.

An idea ran through Stan's mind, something that always made him and his family happy together. Board games! Sure, it was a small thing, but Stan was thinking about the others, so it was worth a shot to at least tell them. He stepped over to a slender oak tree a couple of yards away from the house. He unzipped his slacks and relieved himself, exhaling as he did. It was much better than the bathrooms inside. And Stan knew exactly what he'd do when he got back inside—pull out the Yahtzee board from his briefcase.

The leaves rustled slightly. In the moonlight seeping through the trees, Stan noticed a dark fluid dripping on the bark of the oak he stood behind.

"What's this?" he asked aloud.

Stan zipped his pants back up and ran his fingers across the fluid, streaking them red. As he tried to understand what it truly was, he felt an object land lightly on his shoulders. Stan looked down and grabbed at it, realizing too late that it was a dense rope.

He had no time to react as the noose bucked, pulling him up from the ground. His hands struggled to grasp the rope as black spots started appearing in his vision. He felt his throat being crushed. His feet swayed violently, and he tried to scream. He couldn't make a sound.

The rope continued to rise higher into the trees above. The higher Stan got, the tighter the rope became, despite his frantic efforts to free himself. The lifting motion stopped abruptly. A few more kicks, and Stan's legs stopped moving too. His hands loosened their grip, and his arms dangled down. His eyes fluttered behind the thick-rimmed glasses. A breeze kicked in, and Stan's motionless body wavered in the trees.

15

SPIRITS TAKING OFF

Dinner had ended, and the four in the kitchen retired to the living room, where they all fell onto the couch. Alan flipped the television on. *Saturday Night Fever* was airing. It wasn't a surprise to anyone that Alan loved this movie. He'd seen it numerous times when it was first released. He forgot his worries as he stretched out and placed his arms behind his head to relax.

Tim also settled back. *Saturday Night Fever* was not exactly his cup of tea, but that didn't mean he disliked it. Tim was all right with disco, but if Steve knew about this, he'd smash Alan's television set on impulse.

Rod and Liz cuddled with each other on the couch. Rod had an arm wrapped around Liz's shoulders, watching the movie fixedly; Liz, on the other hand, was more focused on her boyfriend. All of a sudden, she found herself wanting his body.

The couple had been dating for five months, and they hadn't scored yet. She knew Rod had sealed the deal before, but she was still a virgin. Anytime the two kissed, she stopped him before they could go any further. It didn't aggravate Rod or anything. Of course he longed to see his girlfriend's body, but he didn't try to force her or convince her to do anything unless she was ready. One of the reasons she loved Rod was because he didn't mind her waiting; their sleeping together was up to her.

But now, Liz realized that even though Alan and Tim were in the room with them, the way she and Rod were sitting, isolated from the others and cuddling together, was the closest thing to being alone that they'd had in a while. The night before in the Winnebago didn't count; Liz had slept alone in the bed while Rod made his bed in the driver's seat. And in the months earlier, Liz would've never thought about something like sex. But now that their relationship had advanced, she figured she was ready. Also, as good as a friend Tim was at this point, seeing Rod kick him out of the Winnebago had actually been pretty stimulating. Liz would never admit something like that. It wasn't a very kind thing to point out.

"I think I'm going to head upstairs now," Liz said.

Rod turned toward his girlfriend. "Upstairs? You gonna shower or get ready for bed there?"

Liz smiled shyly, shaking her head. "The bathroom is bigger. Besides, it's too early to sleep."

It took Rod a moment to understand, but when he did, his face broke into a cunning grin. Liz gazed down at her lap for a second, moving her leg closer to Rod's. She wasn't giving him eye contact, but only because if she did right now, she'd lose her mind.

"I think when Steve gets back with Tammy, they should have the Winnebago," Liz said.

Rod leaned closer to Liz and whispered in her ear. "And why is that?"

Liz hesitated as she felt herself start to blush. She felt Rod's fingers moving along her thigh, charging her body with a sense of warmth. She felt a little nervous and yet really terrific at the same time.

"Guess." She kissed his cheek.

Her ice-teal eyes met his dark-emerald eyes, and she smiled. It was moments like these that the two felt so in harmony with each other.

"You can come up whenever you'd like," she said, shaking his leg and getting up from the couch. She said good night to Alan and Tim as she went toward the staircase.

The first thing Alan and Tim did was give their pal the silliest-looking grins known to man. They knew exactly what was about to go down. The giveaway was her going upstairs; her bed was supposed to be outside, but it wouldn't have been a good idea to do what the couple planned to accomplish inside of a Winnebago with Steve outside as well. Alan let loose a slight laugh as Rod shook his head and grinned himself.

"I'm getting the hell out of here before you two make me laugh."

Rod headed upstairs—but not before whacking Alan's cap down in front of his face and lightly smacking Tim's arm. Tim reacted with surprise, but Liz had told Rod everything following the altercation the night before. It took Rod a couple of hearings to finally believe her, and seeing that Tim was sort of over it now, he wanted to end the animosity he'd shown his old friend the day before. Rod hated his own guts for attacking his friend over premature, careless accusations.

A cherry aroma hit Rod as he closed the door behind him, locking it to prevent anyone from barging in unexpectedly. Liz bent over to take her shoes off.

"Nice view tonight." Rod moved closer to Liz and grabbed her behind.

Liz gasped and stood straight up with a shoe in one hand. "I ought to hit you with this, you perv."

"I can't help the fact that I enjoyed what I saw." He wrapped his arms around her waist.

"How much did you like what you saw?" Liz teased.

"So...damn...much."

"How much?" She dropped the shoe.

"So..." He leaned closer. "Damn..." Her succulent lips were barely touching his. "Much..."

The two fell onto the bed behind them and began making out. Rod's hands slithered under her olive shirt, grabbing and squeezing her chest tightly. She wrapped her arms around his neck and massaged his shoulders. Then he abruptly stopped.

"Is everything all right?" she asked.

"Yeah, of course it is," Rod replied. "I just want to know one thing: Are you sure you want to do this?"

"I've wondered for months when I'd be ready, Rod. Turns out the wait is over." She grabbed the back of Rod's head and pulled him toward her.

Saturday Night Fever went on commercial break, and Alan returned to the living room with two beers. He handed one to Tim as he took his seat back on the couch.

"Thanks, man." Tim nodded.

"Not a problem." Alan cracked open the can and took a swig of the brew. "Just out of curiosity, Tim, did you have another argument with Veronica earlier?"

"It's that obvious, huh?"

"It's been obvious since we all spent the night at Liz's house. Look—I know Liz is actually a pretty attractive girl, one who can make a guy have sexual thoughts. I may not like her all that much, but I give her credit for that." Alan took another swig. "You want to talk to someone, Tim, then I'm your man. There has to be an actual reason you're suddenly cool with her when I know pretty well that she's been a thorn in your side for months."

The way Alan had asked the question made Tim actually want to answer him. Finally someone wanted to know his side of the story as well. Surprisingly it was Alan, the wisecracker, of all people.

"It started when you guys wanted Liz and me to stay behind and look inside those woods." Tim finally cracked his can open but didn't take a sip. "We started out arguing, but ultimately we sort of got to know each other while out there. Then after Rod wanted us to stay behind at the school, we continued talking. If you get past her voice, her initial personality, and all that stuff, she's not as bad as you think."

"Damn." Alan raised his eyebrows. "That's some heavy shit right there. I know the Timmy Ridges of old would've never responded to Liz like that."

"True." Tim exhaled inaudibly, as Alan had called him Timmy for the first time in a day or so. "Makes me wonder how we'd all be acting with one another if you guys never forced me to stay with her."

"Easy." Alan took a longer mouthful of his brew. "We'd all be acting normal again."

Liz lay under Rod, grasping his waist as he thrust hard into her. The intense feelings she experienced as his warm, slender body moved more rapidly were a panorama of ecstasy, a million fireworks exploding before her eyes. Her tongue twirled inside his mouth for a couple of moments before he moved his mouth to her neck. It turned her on even more than she could possibly have imagined. She felt jittery as the tip of Rod's tongue grazed her neck.

Liz's eyes were shut tight, and all she could see were more lights igniting in her mind. The faster Rod moved, the more numb her lower body became, all the way down to her toes. She moaned hard, her legs clenched around Rod's waist as the heat of the passion engulfed her body. Right as she managed to get him deeper inside of her, Rod climaxed, sending a wave of euphoria that overwhelmed her. She cried out just loudly enough that Rod was the only person who could hear her.

Rod kissed her lips a couple of times as he removed himself from on top of her. He lay back and relaxed, one hand running through his hair and the other arm wrapping around Liz, who wrapped both of hers around him.

The couple shared a smile, relishing in this moment of perfect passion. Neither wanted the moment to end. Liz brushed some tufts of Rod's hair away from his face with her fingers and kissed him gently on the lips.

Liz ran some of her fingers across Rod's chest. Had it been worth the wait? Yes. Did she wish she had done this with him earlier? Maybe. She had such intense emotions just then that she wasn't sure.

But why think of the past when you're in the present—and the present is turning out to be pretty damn good? Liz sat up and lowered her feet to the floor. She got up from the bed and slid her shirt and skirt back on, along with her purple panties.

"Where do you think you're going?" Rod asked with a grin.

"I'm gonna take a shower," Liz giggled. "Just have to get some towels from the Winnebago." She opened the door to walk out but turned back. "You're welcome to join me."

"Good." Rod smirked. "Because I planned on doing so as soon as you mentioned it."

He winked at Liz, who blew a kiss to him as she left the room. Rod caught the kiss, leaning back in bed. He began humming the first verse of "Day In Day Out" by XTC.

Liz hurried downstairs and left the house before Tim and Alan could notice. She waltzed over to the Winnebago, quivering as a cold gust of wind hit her. With her eyes on the Winnebago, she remembered the confrontation the previous night. She sighed and went in.

She retrieved a couple of towels that she'd placed on top of the table by the three-seater shortly after coming back from the lake. As she searched around for the towel bag, she found herself unable to concentrate on anything but Rod. She had a few different thoughts.

The first was simple: the time they'd just spent together. Liz had never felt this kind of elation before. She guessed this was how Veronica felt with Tim. It was such a sensation that Liz wanted to jump back in bed with Rod again. Well, in the shower. Liz felt jittery just thinking about it.

The second thought was a bit more complicated. He hadn't used protection, and she wasn't on the pill. OK, it made sense, at the very least. This was practically spur of the moment, and though Rod had wanted to retrieve a condom from his suitcase, she pulled him back on the bed and pinned him down to keep him for herself. As for Liz, she wasn't on the pill, because she always had a feeling she'd be doing this later on in life. At times she contemplated getting some, just in case she felt she'd be ready at some point, but she'd ended up getting cold feet each time.

She had honestly felt frustrated about her inability to choose whether or not she wanted to sleep with Rod, but now that they had, those feelings were at least put to rest. Still, she came to the conclusion she was going to have to run out sometime to get morning-after pills. If she got pregnant, her parents wouldn't be too happy. And her father would almost certainly want Rod dead...

The third and final thought was the one she actually found to be the worst. Once May rolled around, Rod would be graduating while she would be stuck in Franklin Pierce High for one final year. It killed her to think that they would be apart. Rod had spoken to her before about attending a college in West Virginia just to be close to her. Liz, however, wondered whether Rod, as much as he loved her, would instead want to move away with his friends, people he had known so much longer than her, if they went off to out-of-state schools. Her father would hate this, but she knew she truly loved Rod and didn't want to lose him if he ended up going to a college out of state. Right now everything was fine. They were together and in love. She still had those lingering thoughts, though somehow she had to convince him to stay.

Liz found the cloth towel bag under the table and scooped it up, carrying it in one arm and the towels in the other. Another gust of wind hit her as she climbed out, causing the towel bag to blow out from under her arm before she could place the towels in it. Liz groaned as she watched the bag move along the ground. She could've left it be and returned inside, but her father had the bag imported from Spain for her. She tossed the towels onto the Winnebago's steps and went off after the bag, which tumbled across the grass.

"Just my luck." She sighed.

The cloth bag finally caught on the black steel gates at the entrance of the property. Liz jumped up a couple of times to retrieve the bag, missing it with every leap. Her five-foot-five build wasn't helping. She became impatient; this stupid bag was the only thing keeping her from being back with Rod.

Suddenly the Winnebago lit up behind her, and the engine started. *Someone must be going out,* she thought. She figured it was probably Alan, who needed to stock up on inventory for the following meals, and that maybe he could stop and give her a hand before he left. She heard the camper shift into gear and rev up a bit.

Liz also realized she had to retrieve the towels from the Winnebago before Alan left. Imagine getting the towel bag but forgetting the towels themselves. She heard the camper approach the gate but faster than it should have, as Alan still needed to open the gate to leave. Liz finally caught the bag between her index finger and thumb after making one more forceful jump.

"Gotcha."

Liz's feet never touched the ground. It was only a matter of seconds before the speeding camper, bright headlights shining directly at her, was inches away from her body.

16

OVER AND OVER

Rod sat up in bed and stretched his arms out. He pushed a few tufts of brown hair away from his face, his fingers lined with specks of sweat. He wondered when Liz would be back to the room so they could shower together. Not once did the fact that he'd used no protection bother him.

Instead, Rod thought about how he'd be going to college in five months while his girlfriend remained stuck in Franklin Pierce High for another year. How often would they see each other? Rod didn't know. He didn't even know where he'd be attending college. He promised Liz he'd stay close, somewhere in West Virginia, but what if plans fell through?

Deep down, Rod believed they wouldn't last until August. The two cared for each other a great deal, even if their relationship had started only five months earlier. Hell, Rod cared enough about Liz at this point that he'd be willing to put his life on the line for her. But at the same time, the two of them were total opposites in a lot of ways. Some people say opposites attract. Maybe, but what about *total* opposites?

Liz had been raised in a world of complete wealth her entire life. She'd grown up in a mansion with maids, cooks, and even a butler. That had stopped when she turned thirteen; her parents realized she couldn't have every single thing handed to her. But for the majority of her life, she'd been spoiled excessively. Rod hadn't.

His parents made him work for the stuff he wanted. Rod never argued with them about that, because there wasn't an argument in the first place. Even with all the money his father made working as an executive for a textile company, his family never hired help. Rod and his sister, Michelle, were required to be their own people.

It didn't help that their inner circle of friends were so different from Liz, and her father's total disdain for Rod had pushed him even further from Liz, though he'd never tell anyone. Every day presented a new challenge, some worse than they should've been.

Attacking Tim the night before had been a mistake. Because of the fight and Liz's later explanation of the entire ordeal, Rod hadn't gotten a wink of sleep. Physically fighting his old friend, thinking Tim and Liz were going behind his back—Rod's stomach ached. He stopped going over the situation in his mind. He'd apologize to Tim—case closed.

For the rest of this trip, all the tension needed to stop. Rod committed himself to not losing his temper—which he'd never had until he'd learned his parents were getting a divorce—and just going back to his old self. Calm and complacent.

Stop worrying about everything, he thought. *This is life, and everything in it happens for a reason. Some of it will be amazing; some of it will be a whole ton of bullshit.* Rod declined to contribute more bullshit to the pot.

Rod lay back down on the soft pillow and placed his arms behind his head. He cleared his thoughts to focus on one topic, something he wasn't going to stress about—sex. But Liz still wasn't back yet…

17

AS DARKNESS CLOSES IN

Steve sat at the far edge of the lake. He was tapping the flashlight on his thigh, looking down at the sandy ground and shaking his head. He'd found no sign of Tammy. Not one single piece of evidence that she was anywhere on the grounds.

Steve was more than unnerved at this point. His eyes were closed, and his mouth was shut tight. He tried to remain convinced he'd find her, but now the chances were so damn slim that he was terrified beyond belief. There was no reason why Tammy would wander off and just disappear off the face of the earth.

Steve had a deep thought boiling in the back of his mind that he would not allow himself to believe. Had Tammy been abducted? The words Officer Harold had told him the day before about vandals, arsonists, and thieves didn't help his thought process.

Steve stood up and froze. The officer had mentioned something about recent deaths in the area, but what was it? His knees buckled as he remembered. Officer Harold had gotten a call—three bodies were found somewhere in the area.

It was no longer something to take lightly. Tammy might not have been playing a game with him after all. Steve felt sick. Then the adrenaline hit him. He had to get back on his feet and go inside to call the police and file a missing-persons report. It was urgent. Tammy could be in trouble, and calling the cops was the only possible way he could quickly get help from people who actually knew the area.

Steve had heard so many legends about these kinds of horrific events. All of them had to do with a homicidal psychopath who either murdered everyone or was defeated and killed by the hero.

Steve wanted to be the latter. And in order to do that, he needed to get out of the woods and back inside. No, he didn't have any evidence that Tammy was dead—or that there even was a killer. But he knew it wasn't safe anymore; this vacation had taken a turn. As Steve ran, his heart beat faster with every rustle of the leaves and every branch his foot snapped. Just being in the woods in general made his heart palpitate faster.

Could it be Ray Kuiper? That was the stupidest thing to be thinking right now, but what if had been? He could have been waiting in the darkness to leap out at Steve, screaming and tackling him to the ground, pulling out a knife and doing God knows what.

Worse yet, could it have been one of the group? Steve knew damn well everyone thought of Tammy with the utmost infuriation. It was a sure possibility something could've happened to Tammy while he'd been asleep; the murderer might even be inside the lake house, waiting for the right time to kill.

The more Steve accelerated toward where the path around the lake began, the more he feared for the lives of those inside the house. He had a strong gut feeling that if someone in the group was a killer, it was Rod.

He wasn't the same guy Steve had gone to kindergarten with all those years ago. Everything about him had suddenly changed. He was more aggressive, more prone to random outbursts of anger.

The more Steve pondered Rod's so-called new personality, the worse his stomach felt. He finally made it to the beginning of the path and breathed a sigh of relief that part one of his trek had ended. Now all he had to do was walk through the door and see what was to come there. Steve worked his way along the path between bushes on each side. The first thing he noticed was that the Winnebago was no longer by the entrance.

"Shit," Steve mumbled, trying to imagine the vehicle still placed before the house. He began to run toward the front door, but he tripped over a strange object. Steve fell face-first onto the dirt and turned himself over, wiping grime from his mouth.

The moment Steve's flashlight hit what he had fallen over, everything stopped. It was a body. Steve was speechless as he saw Stan's lifeless purple face framed in a hangman's noose. He swallowed hard, unable to take his eyes off Stan's body. Was he seeing things? Was his brain playing tricks on him? Steve recoiled and jumped back to his feet. Before he could run to the door, he saw the Winnebago out of the corner of his left eye.

It couldn't be; this couldn't be. Steve turned and pointed the flashlight to his left. The Winnebago was smashed into the gates, right where a swing set once had stood. Steve didn't want to investigate it, but he felt he had to.

He was still in shock, trying to cope with what he had just seen. It had to be a hoax, a sick prank. Steve charged over to the Winnebago and stopped near it.

"Guys, please answer me. This fucking shit isn't funny." Steve walked around the side and up to the front of the vehicle.

His body turned cold, and his face was as pale as a ghost. The sight that greeted him was so horrifying, so grisly, and so gruesome that he gagged immediately. It appeared to be Liz, her body crushed so hard between the Winnebago and the entrance gate that her body, or what was left of it, nearly sliced through the gate. The gate was dripping with blood, and pieces of her chest flesh were embedded in it. Her teal eyes were still open and staring straight up into the sky. One arm was nowhere to be seen, but the other sagged to her side. Steve saw nothing at all of her lower body. Blood leaked from her gaping mouth and down her lips and chin. It was the bloodiest sight he had ever seen.

Steve dashed from the Winnebago to the front door and banged on it recklessly and furiously. The door swung open a moment later, courtesy of Tim.

"Steve! What the hell is going on?" Tim grabbed Steve's shoulders.

Steve hugged his friend as he kicked the door closed behind him. He began to shake.

"Steve, come on. Answer me!"

"What's going on?" Alan asked, exiting the kitchen.

Steve let go of Tim and backed up to the door. He gulped. Rod came running down the stairs.

"S-Stan and L-Liz are d-dead..." Steve crossed his arms tightly. He was about to throw up; his stomach churned viciously.

"What the hell are you talking about?" Rod cocked an eyebrow.

Tim and Alan didn't say anything. Steve started to breathe in and out forcefully. He'd seen the sights; he wouldn't make up something like that. Claiming people were dead was a serious matter, and if Steve *was* kidding, he'd really be in for it.

"You don't believe me? Then check outside! Stan had a fucking noose wrapped around his neck, and Liz...God, what's left of Liz is crushed between my fucking Winnebago and the fence outside!" Steve yelled.

Rod shoved Steve out of the way and opened the door over Tim's and Alan's protests. He stopped, staring outside at the Winnebago pushed all the way up by the gate.

Rod backed inside and shut the door. His girlfriend was dead? His girlfriend, Elizabeth Carlough, was dead? Rod moved over to the couch and clamped his eyes shut to process it all. A single tear ran down his cheek, followed by a few more. Steve began to tear up as well. Liz and Stan were people too; they weren't his favorite people, but that didn't matter.

Alan realized his fears were legitimate and remembered Richie still wasn't around. He darted into the room down the hall and busted open the locked door as Veronica rushed down the stairs, having been awoken by all the commotion.

"What's going on?" Veronica asked.

"Veronica"—Tim put his arms around his girlfriend as Steve comforted Rod—"stay here with us. We're calling the police."

"What for?" she asked, shocked.

Tim could barely speak. "Liz and Stan—they—they're d-dead…"

Veronica froze, opening her mouth but not speaking. How else was she supposed to react? She fell into Tim's arms as Alan came back out of the room, close to freaking out. He took his hat off to wipe away some sweat from his forehead.

"R-Richie's gone." Alan panted.

"And where the hell is Tammy?" Steve screamed, sliding down the door to the ground.

"Tim, call the police," Alan ordered as he dashed to the bar in the back.

Tim followed Alan, one arm still wrapped around Veronica, who began trembling, her big blue eyes glassy. As Tim picked up the phone, Alan materialized from behind the bar, swiftly putting bullets inside a Smith and Wesson Model 29 as though he had done this before.

"Where the hell did you get that?" Tim stared at the handgun.

"It's my father's," Alan stated. "Now hurry up and call the damn cops."

Tim put the phone to his ear and began dialing, but he didn't hear any sounds on the line. He looked at the handset for a second and then set it back on the hook before returning it to his ear. Still no sound. "No. Don't tell me the phone lines are down." Tim slammed the phone on the receiver.

Alan smacked the bullet chamber shut.

"H-how are we going to get out of here?" Rod stammered, walking with a crestfallen Steve toward the others.

A crash resonated from upstairs, and everyone jumped abruptly. Alan suddenly kicked one of the barstools in rage. The flying wooden stool smacked onto the floor, and a leg broke off. Someone was inside Alan's room.

"That was a five-thousand-dollar vase!"

Rod impulsively darted up the stairs. An assailant was up there—the being who'd slaughtered his girlfriend. Rod wasn't letting him get away. Tim and Steve attempted to grab him.

"Rod, don't!" Veronica screamed.

"You'll get yourself killed!" Tim shouted.

And before the others knew it, Steve dashed away from the group and went off after Rod. The two guys found themselves at the top of the staircase on the third story. The sole room, Alan's, was to the right. The door was slightly ajar.

Rod pushed it open slowly. Steve looked downstairs for a moment and saw the three others huddled together below. Alan had his revolver ready. Steve took a deep breath.

"I'm going to find this piece of shit. I'm not going to stop until I do," Rod whispered. "I'll tear this room apart. This person is going to take Liz's death to the grave, and so might I. Whoever's in here killed her, and I'd give my life to avenge her."

There was no more time for jokes or relaxation anymore. Coming out alive was the only goal. Somehow, someway, they were going to leave alive. Whatever it took. The two snuck inside.

"I thought I'd check out your place since you were kind enough to stop by mine," a voice said in a distinct South African accent.

Fear set in. Adrenaline coursed through the boys' bodies.

"Who—" Steve began.

The light turned on from the pull of a chain. Before the two teenagers was a man sitting like Buddha on the golden sheets of Alan's neatly made bed. He had long dark hair, wet and slicked back; a scruffy beard; and a sinister grin. He wore a black tank top, tan pants, and black army boots. He was not an imposing figure height-wise, but his overall frame was muscular.

"My name…is Ray Kuiper." The man rubbed his hands together. "'Who is Ray Kuiper?' you might ask yourself. Some may think of me as a hunter. Others tend to think of me as a psychopath."

Steve and Rod remained frozen in silence.

"I do consider myself a hunter of sorts. I enjoy the thrill of the chase. Remorse is not a strong suit of mine, but shamelessness is one of my favorite traits."

Steve trembled ever so slightly.

"When I hunt, I don't stop until all the prey in the area have become my trophies. And I don't mean deer antlers. Animals are child's play. If you don't believe me, this will surely change your opinion."

Kuiper retrieved an oval-shaped object from behind him on the bed.

"It was once a man, in case you wish to know."

The object was a head; it had little hair in light-brown patches and tufts. And then there was what could loosely be described as a face. Its flesh was peeling off, revealing an undercoating of bright-red and charred-purple skin oozing blood and liquid. The boys gagged at the grotesque sight; it would be burned in their minds forever. Kuiper cackled devilishly, his eyes wide in amusement.

"A severed head!" Kuiper shouted.

Rod shoved Steve out of the bedroom.

"Go, Steve! Get the others and run!" Rod ordered.

Steve stayed put. Part of him wanted to help his old friend—possibly save him from death. If they failed, however, there still may have been hope for the three others. They knew there was an intruder and Alan had a gun. But Steve couldn't leave Rod in the room with a maniac, a legend come to life. Despite all of what he'd thought earlier, Steve didn't want Rod to be killed.

"Go! Now!" Rod yelled.

Steve closed his eyes for a split second. There was nothing left for him to do. Unwillingly and guiltily, Steve darted down the stairs as Rod rushed deeper into the bedroom. Steve's heart was ready to flee from his chest. This was a mistake. He should've stayed there and helped Rod, the brave one. Rod's willingness to risk his life for the others gave Steve a newfound respect for him. Rod refused to let his pals die.

"Where the hell is Rod?" Veronica grabbed Steve's arms.

A scream from upstairs echoed throughout the house. Seconds later, the bedroom door burst open, and Rod came crashing out with the broken wooden door behind him.

"What the fuck?" Alan raised the revolver upward.

No one saw Ray Kuiper appear from the room. They only saw Rod's body lifted up and flung from over the third-story railing. He crashed back first through the glass coffee table. Rod's body thrashed violently before becoming still. Then the three heard footsteps descending the staircase.

Veronica screamed. Alan's hands struggled to keep the gun pointed toward the stairs. His hands shook so nervously that he lost his grip on the revolver and the gun crashed to the floor.

"The game begins right now," Kuiper growled.

The teenagers soon saw his army boots on the steps. They took no chances; they raced out the front door, grasping the fact that they all might die tonight. Alan forgot the revolver.

There was no way they'd be able to get help at this point. It was them against Ray Kuiper, a self-professed hunter. The outcome was clear as day: March 12, 1980, would be the day everything turned red.

18

PHANTASMAGORIA

R ay Kuiper stood at the open door, watching the four teenagers disappear into the darkness. He clasped his fingers, turning his hands inside out to crack them. Undoing the black wrapping tape around his right wrist a bit, he found a small blade still intact in case he needed to use it. Or wanted to use it. Pain did nothing to him; the few strikes he'd received from Rod may as well have been from a feather. Fury was captured in the hunter's glowering eyes.

Every decade, someone curious would hear his story and look into the mystery regarding his "death." And it was no coincidence that those who discovered his legend or investigated the circumstances surrounding his disappearance turned up dead. He'd find ways to figure out who'd been looking into him. That sealed the death wish, whether it happened to be a single person or an entire group.

Kuiper thought back to his time at Franklin Pierce High School in 1952. It had been only a little crush; everyone had known he'd never go anywhere with it. Lust would have been a more accurate definition. Every day he worked hard at the movie theater, wanting to buy the perfect rose and an expensive suit so he could take the girl of his dreams to the upcoming winter formal. It took four months of hard work, but he completed the task. By November, he had his black tuxedo and crisp white dress shirt.

But one day, the young usher greeted the object of his affection at the movie theater. Finally he was so close to saying hello to her, to asking her the question to which he'd been longing to get an answer. And then a boy came up and put an arm around her waist. Kuiper was devastated. It turned out to be one of the only people who had ever bothered to give Kuiper the time of day: Robert Leeds, a friend since middle school.

Otherwise he felt all but ignored by the entire student body. He was an outsider, treated with contempt. One day, after pondering whether his peers would remember him as they parted ways come graduation, the boy came to one simple conclusion.

People would care—if he went missing. Missing teenagers always got sympathy; it was foolproof. He figured that upon his return, the town would hold massive celebrations for the missing boy who had come back unharmed. His parents, though loving, would be forced to learn of his plan the hard way when he didn't return home after school one afternoon.

That same fateful day, he entered the basement of the school to get supplies for a teacher. He continued to work out the plan in his mind as he retrieved a box of chemicals and acid from a high shelf. Everything changed when a fellow student entered the basement. This boy always laughed at Kuiper, whether it was because of his thick South African accent or because he had a fascination with his home country.

Today Ray Kuiper had had enough of this type of bullshit. When the boy insulted his family and heritage, Kuiper snapped. Without thinking, he slammed the box against the other boy's head, sending him tumbling to the ground. Jumping off the chair he'd been standing on, Kuiper kicked his foot underneath it, sending it flying up and into his hands. He slammed the chair against the other boy's back before flinging it across the room. Then he saw the acid container roll out of the box.

It was a sign. Kuiper retrieved the container of acid and, donning the first of what would become many maniacal grins, shattered the beaker against the boy's skull.

Kuiper forgot everything else that had happened that day. He woke up in the woods that night feeling drowsy and shivering from the cold weather. He remembered the attack, however, and initially felt a tinge of regret. He was unable to believe at first that he'd assaulted another human being. And he decided there was no way in hell he could ever show his face in Charleston, let alone the school, again after such an event. In just seconds, Ray Kuiper's life had fallen apart, and he found himself driven to insanity.

He remained deep in the woods, carefully hidden from the world around him. Stolen newspapers revealed the boy had survived his attack but suffered severe burns on the top of his head. Though the boy never disclosed who the assailant was, because of a loss of memory after the attack, Kuiper had no doubt people would point their fingers toward him. But it didn't matter. He was officially declared dead in 1953, barely a year after his disappearance.

The following year, the students of Franklin Pierce High School began to tell one another tall tales about the incident. They stayed faithful at first to the story, but the more it was told, the more it morphed into a new entity. The new story found Kuiper himself burned to death in a chemical wastebasket, and he now somehow had a secret to tell.

If that wasn't enough, the teenagers who told the legend raised the bar by explaining the whole ordeal was a cover-up by the high school and the state government. If only they had given him more attention. If only they had treated him more like a friend than an outsider. Such platitudes made Kuiper fume when he learned about them.

He thought these teenagers brought this entirely upon themselves. They'd intruded on his shed in the woods. Kuiper had no idea they were the children of some of the people he had gone to school with. To him, they were only more prey to be hunted. And no one would find them; no one would hear them when they screamed.

Kuiper's arsenal sat just a few yards away inside the wrecked Winnebago. He picked up the revolver Alan had left behind; it was yet another weapon he could use. Stalking toward the vehicle, he thought about elaborate ways to kill his soon-to-be victims. With the right weapon—a speargun—he had his targets right where he wanted them. The lake house and Private Property X were the only places in the general area. They couldn't run for long. All prey gave up at some point.

19

IT CAN'T BE...

The night air had a sudden fog to it. The sky wasn't cloudy, but the stars that had shone brightly overhead were nowhere to be seen, unable to watch with their sparkling eyes all that took place. It would have been impossible for Tim, Steve, Veronica, and Alan to describe the feelings they were experiencing at the moment.

They ran faster than they ever had as a madman stalked their every move. That's what happens when the adrenaline gets pumping. On impulse, Alan grabbed Steve's shoulder to let him know he was taking a left.

Soon everyone swerved in the same direction. Alan, now the pack leader, raced to get himself and his friends to safety. He knew where to go. Private Property X. The trek would be a treacherous one, but Alan remembered a shortcut. He brought them through the bushes and shrubs onto a path that led down to the lake. As long as they kept running, not stopping and looking behind them, they'd be safe. The killer no longer stood at the door.

The lake was in sight, and the moon gave the four needed light. They'd been in such a rush that they'd forgotten the flashlights inside the lake house. The lights on the patio suddenly turned on. An object shot through the window, shattering the glass, and tumbled down a steep drop toward the lake.

It looked like a body. Alan stopped quickly and approached it. He almost had a mental breakdown when he recognized the body—Richie, his throat slashed violently and spewing blood.

"No!" Alan yelled. "Richie!"

Alan stared at the patio. He had no time to react when a trigger clicked, and a spear zoomed through the air straight toward him. It penetrated Alan's stomach within seconds, like a detonation. He screamed in agony as the force of the impact sent him flying into the lake behind him.

For first time that night, Tim and Steve broke down completely. Alan's life ended right before their eyes. One of their oldest pals was dead, along with Richie. The fact that Alan had found Richie's body just seconds before his own demise made the pain stronger. Veronica's knees buckled as she screamed shrilly.

But somehow they found themselves able to resume running. It was just them now, and their own lives were just as important. The fog got thicker as they traveled farther down the path. Soon the three teenagers lost track of one another as they fled deeper into the fog.

Tim ran one way while Steve and Veronica sprinted another. He had no idea where they were heading. The one thing he knew was that death was closing in on all of them. It was a race against time; when time expired, so would they.

Tears blinded Veronica's eyes. It was too much for her to handle. She didn't feel as strong as Tim or Steve. But how else was she supposed to act when some of her closest friends had just died right before her eyes? The emotional pain spread throughout her body like a wildfire, but that didn't stop her from running. It was what the others would've told her to do. Veronica was sure Tim and Steve weren't in front of or behind her, but she tried to be hopeful.

I can make it out of here without Tim, she told herself. But could she go on by herself? She wouldn't dare. Veronica knew she would rather die than leave her boyfriend and friend out in the woods alone to fend for themselves.

Lost in her thoughts, she didn't see the fallen branch resting in the path. It took one trip, and Veronica collided with the sandy dirt ground. She tumbled down a steep incline and splashed into the lake.

Steve's trail found him going up a slope. He had gone far enough up-hill to be able to see some lights emerging from a clearing. Though tired from all the running, Steve staggered to the entrance. It was a sheer ascent, and he lost his balance twice. He used what remained of his strength to climb two steps. He moved forward cautiously until he reached the clearing.

But now he was confused. He stood before what seemed to be a maze of five dozen tall, misshapen, and misplaced wood fences. Above the fences stood six massive streetlights, positioned unusually and shining on the dirt below.

Steve made his way to one of the fences and looked around. No one was in sight, and he didn't know where he was or where these fences led—if anywhere.

Sweat from his bangs dripped into his widened eyes, temporarily blinding him as he raced through the fences, scarcely climbing over a couple and swerving through others. His worn-out body moved more slowly, and he had to keep himself aware. The psychopath lurked any-where. Even the glow from the streetlights didn't mean he was safe.

Steve's paranoia about the situation became so unhealthy that he stopped running. He crept around the fences, peeking around each corner to see whether the killer stood there, waiting for him to be-come prey. After he passed a few more fences, Steve gave in to his growing fatigue and leaned against one of them to catch his breath.

Running in the cold air had made Steve's mouth dry and his ears numb. He took three deep breaths and closed his eyes for a second. He didn't notice a hand reach around the corner of the fence until it clenched his neck, grabbing him by the throat. He yelped in horror and then croaked.

Instinctively his hands flew up and grabbed one of the psychopath's, trying to rip himself from the grip. It didn't work. Ray Kuiper walked with ease through the maze and made a clean exit, moving toward a damaged house. Steve assumed this was the Private Property X Alan had talked about. By now Kuiper's entire arm clasped Steve's neck, dragging him along. Steve tried kicking—anything to loosen the grip. Death seemed inevitable.

Soon the killer kicked the door to the house open and hauled Steve up to the second story. Pieces of glass, wood, and bricks were strewn about the otherwise empty building. Boards covered the windows, and the ceiling appeared to be falling down.

The killer pinned Steve to the wall and grabbed his throat once more, lifting him up from the ground. With his available hand, Kuiper unsheathed a hunting knife from a tool belt and jammed it into Steve's right thigh to prevent him from running.

Searing-hot pain engulfed Steve's thigh as he screamed in anguish. The killer released him from his grip, and Steve sensed his body fall to the ground, his eyes watching the area where the knife had impaled him. Warm blood seeped through his jeans and flowed down his leg.

Darkness did not cloak the room; rays from the streetlights emerged through the boards covering the window. It was convenient for the psychopath, as the light shone in such a way that Ray was able to keep an eye on Steve, but Steve wasn't able to anticipate further blows.

As Steve writhed on the floor, Kuiper went over to the corner of the dark room, flicking a switch. It didn't light up the entire room, just a shelved area. Steve gazed over at the light, and everything stopped.

A severed head appeared on the single shelf, the light shining above it. It was the head of a teenage girl, blood splattered all over her face. A phrase was carved into the wall behind the shelf. Steve had seen that phrase before: "Nothing will remain the same," the exact words carved into the wall of the custodian house behind Franklin Pierce High School two days earlier.

"This pretty trophy is all that's left of your little girlfriend." Kuiper grinned, caressing the severed head. "And you'll never find the rest of her body."

Steve felt like his heart had stopped momentarily, and his entire body stiffened. Everything he'd hoped for was put to rest. His eyes locked on the head. Tammy's head. Memories of the last moment he'd spent with her swarmed through his mind. Steve's mouth shuddered intensely, and he fell onto his side, unable to keep himself from letting tears loose.

Tim heard screams to his right. They sent chills down his spine; he knew they were Steve's. He changed his route and ran uphill toward the sound. He just missed tripping as he appeared at the top of the knoll and glanced at the same sight Steve had seen when he came to the lit clearing.

Tim didn't question the bizarre fence setup. He wanted to know how he would get through them. One mistake, and Steve might be dead. And what about Veronica?

Thinking about all the possibilities of Veronica's whereabouts sent a rush of intensity through Tim's body as his feet picked up speed through the fences. Every couple of turns, his eyes scanned around, making sure he was alone and that chances of an ambush were low. He made a final turn and stood at the end of the fences.

In front of him stood the damaged house. The streetlights brought out the chipping gray paint of the house, the sloppy boards on the windows, and the faded-green door.

It was a horrid, eerie sight. Tim had seen abandoned houses before but nothing of this caliber. He went up to the door, still looking around for any sign of Kuiper. A piece of metal clanging against steel rang in his ears. Tim's eyes focused back on the door, and he pushed it open.

Without the beams of light entering through the boarded windows, everything would've been obscured. Tim attempted to follow the rays, trying his best to sneak around as quietly as possible. But everywhere he stepped, his feet crushed pieces of glass. His heavy breathing, a result of all the running, was the most prevalent noise in the otherwise silent room.

"Steve?" Tim stood by one of windows. "Steve?" His voice came out quiet, above a whisper.

Tim walked a few steps, trying to get over to another window. Out of nowhere, he tripped over a piece of brick and slammed to the concrete, but he got back on his feet with ease and approached the next window. He looked up.

"Steve?"

No response. Tim turned to move away and heard a creaking noise—the sound of the ceiling caving in little by little. Tim flinched when some dust landed on his head, almost jumping from the sudden fright. Then he heard someone yelling from above.

"Steve?" Tim's voice was still too quiet for anyone to hear.

Tim followed the voice, and his feet bumped into what he found to be the staircase. He took every step up carefully, not just because of the darkness but also because the rickety staircase looked like it could give at any moment. If that wasn't disturbing enough, the staircase had no railing. This meant the farther Tim moved up, the longer the potential fall. Another yell echoed through the house. Tim took his final step at the top—just as all the lights in the house activated.

The first thing Tim saw in the light was Ray Kuiper's face plastered with a terrifying grin. Tim leaped back, sending him tumbling down the staircase and onto the concrete below. Ray held an immense tree trimmer, which he started up without hesitation.

"Tim!" Steve shouted from upstairs.

Kuiper descended with the tree trimmer, its sharp rotary blade spinning faster than it appeared. Tim stumbled to his feet as the killer hit the bottom step, swiping the trimmer at him. He evaded all the swings with little effort, using side movements and some ducks, until he tripped over another misplaced brick.

"Fucking bricks!" Tim yelled as he crawled backward, moving away from the approaching killer.

Kuiper momentarily stopped the tree trimmer, but only so Tim could hear his petrifying words. "Nowhere to run, cornered by the hunter." Kuiper smiled hysterically. "You express fear; I express thrill. And when the hunter has his eyes on the prize, the prey becomes another trophy on display."

Tim couldn't move back much more. He came up to the corner of a wall. He was trapped completely, unable get away. Tim's life was over. He hadn't realized it until this moment, and his life flashed before his eyes.

"This will only take a second." Kuiper pulled the lever of the tree trimmer again.

The weapon moved closer and closer to Tim's stomach. It would tear open in just a matter of seconds. Kuiper readied for the perfect execution. The ferocious noise coming from the tree trimmer got louder. Tim clenched his eyes shut—but not before he caught Steve out the corner of them.

Steve had removed the knife from his thigh and wobbled down the stairs with the last of his strength. He raised the knife above his head and threw the blade directly toward Kuiper. It lodged straight into his back.

Kuiper winced, gasping. He turned around and swung the tree trimmer at Steve. He nearly got away, but the rotary blade struck him in his left thigh, the unwounded one. Steve screamed, falling onto his back and grabbing his thigh, his eyes squinting tight. Tim saw a miraculous chance now. As Kuiper focused only on Steve, Tim jumped up and shoved his palm against the handle of the knife embedded in Kuiper's back.

The killer grunted, dropping the tree trimmer from his hands. It landed right between Steve's legs, the sudden surprise immobilizing

Steve's entire body. Kuiper fell onto his knees and went straight down, red liquid seeping down his back. His right hand reached behind him, swinging wildly for the knife, and he clenched his teeth. Tim rushed around the fallen attacker and grabbed Steve's hand, carefully dragging him over to the door.

The tree trimmer rested on the ground and continued to spin, creating a horrible screeching noise as the blade rotated against the concrete. Lifting Steve to his feet, Tim put his arm around his friend and carried him to the door. The wounds to his legs looked drenched with blood but thankfully not too grave.

Swinging the door open, the two teenagers found themselves face-to-face with Veronica. She'd followed the sounds of screaming, as Tim had, after getting out of the lake. Drenched from head to toe, she had small cuts up her arms, and a mild scrape decorated her left cheek. Her appearance brought another fright to the two boys, but that alarm shifted into elation. They all embraced one another, crying tears of joy. Then everyone saw the body of Ray Kuiper rising up from the ground. He pulled the knife from his back and licked the blood from the blade.

"Stop!" Veronica broke free of the embrace, rushing into the room.

She retrieved the tree trimmer and swung it. The rotary blade slashed the man across the stomach in a flash. Blood spurted out of his wound and straight onto Veronica's face. She continued swinging the tree trimmer upward, slicing his chest open. As she turned the weapon off and threw it to the floor, Kuiper's eyes locked with hers. He knew someone with that same distinctive face. On an impulse, he grabbed her shoulders.

"S-S-Susan?" he stuttered.

"S-Susan?" Veronica stammered.

Her mother, Tim thought, unable to say the words aloud.

"Take care." Kuiper's eyes rolled into the back of his head.

Ray Kuiper landed on the concrete, blood streaming out of his chest and stomach. The tatters of his ruined tank top exposed blood-soaked flesh and muscle. The knife fell from his hands. Veronica, her skin prickled with goose bumps, shrieked and rushed into Tim's open arms. Tim quickly led the others out of the house. But where were they to go? A sharp wind picked up, and another figure emerged, this one coming from the maze of fences. It couldn't be. Rod.

He hobbled over to the others, his body weakened from his flight over the railing. He, like the others, couldn't believe he was still alive. Rod stared down the others for a moment, but he moved in and embraced them all. Their ordeal was over, yet it was no victory. Events like this had no victories, no winners.

20

UP AND DOWN

March 18, 1980

Funerals made Tim cringe inside. He had been to one funeral, that of his paternal grandfather. But it had been years ago, and he had blocked out the memory. The word *funeral* brought two simple pictures to mind: dead bodies and sad people. This one proved different, though.

Anytime a sixteen-year-old girl is brutally murdered, it just makes people want to understand why. At some points, Tim even questioned, "Why them?" and "Why us?" but it wasn't healthy to think that way. It'd bring self-pity.

The day had a somber atmosphere, and gray clouds filled the sky. A few people dotted East Grove Cemetery. Some were visiting graves; some were just taking walks. The majority, however, loomed in one spot, where a hazel casket perched by a tombstone. The casket stood out from the people all around, dressed in black attire.

It was a closed-casket funeral, at the request of Liz's parents. The sight of her body, or what remained of it, would have invoked horror. This was a time to praise her life, not dwell over the cause of her death. People all around cried, most of them silently. Only Mrs. Carlough bawled hysterically. No one blamed her.

Tim stood among the others, motionless as the priest spoke from the New Testament. Steve rested on crutches to his right, aviator shades covering his bloodshot eyes. The crutches were wedged firmly under both arms, as the leg wounds Steve had received left him barely able to stand. His face was still and blank.

Veronica stood at Tim's left, a black pillbox hat adorning her head. She wiped some tears away with a handkerchief. Steve and Veronica may not have cared all too much for Liz, but they'd never wanted something like this to happen to her.

Liz wasn't the only recent victim buried at East Grove. All the deceased friends rested there, or would; Richie's funeral would take place the following Tuesday.

"Let us commend Elizabeth Marie Carlough to the mercy of God," the priest said among the weeping.

He said two or three prayers, commending Liz for her life on earth. And then the most painful part of the entire ceremony occurred: the lowering of her casket into the grave.

"We therefore commit her body to the ground—earth to earth, ashes to ashes, dust to dust—in the sure and certain hope of the resurrection to eternal life."

Tim turned his head away; the emotions proved too much to bear. Veronica held on to his arm, while Steve's mouth trembled. Seconds later, it ended. The mourners dispersed before the casket disappeared from sight. Aside from the three, all the others went back to their cars.

Liz's mother continued to bawl, and Mr. Carlough wrapped an arm around her shoulder to comfort her. Tim glanced out over the rest of the cemetery and saw a figure observing everything from a distance. It was Rod.

He wore an all-black suit and stood straight, his left hand resting in the pocket of his slacks and his right arm enclosed in a sling. The fall from the railing had shattered bones in his upper arm.

"I'll be back in a second," Tim whispered.

"Where are you going?" Veronica asked, surprised.

Tim pointed to Rod's figure standing in the distance. Veronica nodded, but she didn't ask to go with him. It was to be the first time Tim and Rod had talked to each other since the event.

"All right," Steve said, not turning to look at Tim, his eyes watching the gravediggers shovel dirt over the casket.

Tim headed over toward Rod. He stood by a tombstone marked with the name Edgar on it. He'd kept his distance from the other mourners because Liz's father had refused to allow him to attend the funeral. Mr. Carlough held Rod responsible for everything, and Rod didn't fight him on that point. Both Mr. Carlough and Rod believed they could have prevented the death of the girl they both loved and yet failed to do so. However, Mr. Carlough was powerless to bar him from going to the cemetery on that day.

"Rodney," Tim said.

"Timothy."

"How are things?"

"Shitty. You?"

"Been better myself."

"I'm sorry to hear that."

Tim hesitated for a moment, his eyes wandering back to the sight of Liz's grave and to Steve and Veronica talking to each other a couple of yards away. He turned back to Rod, staring down at the cleanly cut grass.

"She would've wanted you here. Liz."

"You think so?"

"If it wasn't for Mr. Carlough and his delusional idea that you're the one responsible, you would've been here."

"I suppose you're right," Rod responded, "but I'm still not sure if I would've gone regardless. It was bad enough attending Alan's funeral and even Tammy's memorial service. And life's just been hell."

"I get what you mean," Tim acknowledged. "And what you're going through too."

"And I want to apologize," Rod continued. "For every single thing I did at that lake house. I don't know what got into me. Everything seemed to be tearing me apart, trying to deal with the hardships of my parents' marriage breaking down. And when I saw you with Liz that night in the Winnebago, I assumed I would lose her too. And if that had happened, what would be left in the life of Rod Grandt?" He shrugged. "Instead I lost Liz in the only way I never expected. As for you, Tim, I should've known better. We've been friends since kindergarten, and you've been nothing but a great friend throughout everything."

"Rod," Tim began, "I forgive you. You've had the roughest time the past few months, and everything you did, as crazy as it was, is still understandable considering the emotions going through you."

Rod smiled. It was the first smile that had crossed his face in so long that he'd almost forgotten how to do it. Tim returned the gesture.

"Thanks." Rod took his hand out of his pocket and patted Tim on the shoulder.

Veronica and Steve made their way over. Veronica and Steve kept in touch with Rod, if not as much as usual.

"Hey, Rod," Steve remarked.

"Hey, Steven."

"How are you?" Veronica hugged Rod in a gentle embrace so as not to hurt his broken arm.

"I'm doing fine." Rod looked at his surroundings. "You never can say you're doing well when you're at a cemetery."

"True," Tim agreed.

Rod pulled a long-stemmed red rose from his jacket pocket. "If you'll excuse me for a second."

Rod made his way to Liz's grave. The others stayed where they were, watching him. He stopped directly in front of the headstone, his head drooped completely. As Rod stood before her grave, he read her name.

"Elizabeth Marie Carlough," he stated, staring at the headstone intently. "I'll always miss you and cherish the months we spent to-gether." He gulped hard. "I loved you so much, yet as time went on, you seemed so far away. I called you things I should be damned for, and I just wish you could still be here with me. I—I wish this wasn't how it had to end…"

As Tim, Steve, and Veronica approached him, Rod placed the rose before the headstone. He heard the footsteps approaching him and turned around.

"I should go now," Rod said. "I'll see you guys later." He waved and walked away. Tim wished he could've stayed longer with them, but that proved impossible. The cemetery broke him into pieces, and his staying there would have made everything worse.

The others waved to him and watched their friend depart. Rod needed all the time possible to control his emotions. Because of that, the three never really saw much of their old friend from that point on.

With barely anyone left in the cemetery, it was time for them to leave. They headed out of the cemetery and to the parking lot. Tim's Pontiac Trans Am was one of the only cars there. Veronica's fingers intertwined with her boyfriend's, and Tim placed his hand on Steve's shoulder. They all felt the closest they had been in months. It's strange how death brings people together.

No one said a word the entire ride, much like the one to the cemetery an hour before. Tim appeared to be deep in thought, yet nothing crossed his mind. Veronica noticed this but didn't say a word. Steve sat in the back, staring out the window.

When the search parties couldn't locate the rest of Tammy's body, Steve had forced himself to come to terms with the reality that there really was no way he could've saved her. He had attended Tammy's memorial service a few days earlier. Tim and Veronica had gone along to support him, regardless of their feelings toward Tammy. The pain struck Steve so much that he hated it if someone even mentioned her name. He'd cared for Tammy, even if their time together ended up being brief. In Steve's mind, she wasn't just a fling.

And to top everything off was the most tormenting part. Ray Kuiper: In barely three days, he'd gone from being a fun diversion—a macabre legend—to a psychopathic hunter. Kuiper chased them like it was a game. The teenagers were the ones who ended his "entertainment." Tim had been sure he'd never see another day—as he ran through the area surrounding the lake house—but then he found himself sitting on the couch in his house. The events were so traumatizing that no one wished to speak Kuiper's name aloud. It'd only bring back memories of the night.

Some could even question whether the man truly was Ray Kuiper. Tim had seen the photos, read the articles, and knew the story. Without a doubt, the man they'd encountered had to be Ray Kuiper—or a man committed to making the legend a reality by learning the story and making it his own.

At the snap of a finger, the thirty-minute ride ended, and Tim parked the black-and-gold Trans Am in his driveway. The three exited the car slowly as a breeze picked up. Tim realized a breeze came out of the blue whenever he and others were miserable. Bizarre.

"Hey, Tim!" a high-pitched voice called.

"Li—" Tim looked down the street, but no one appeared. It must've been the breeze playing games with him.

Tim had been hearing voices in his mind since he'd come back from the lake house. He'd hear Liz's complaints, Alan's joking, and Richie's sly comments day in and day out. Sometimes even Stan's and Tammy's voices rang in his head.

Tim opened the door to his house and walked in. Steve and Veronica followed close behind. As Veronica closed the door, Tim's parents descended the staircase and noticed the sullen teenagers. His parents hugged them, comforting them in the only way they knew how.

"Tim, your father and I are going out. But unless you'd like some company—"

"We can manage." Tim leaned in and kissed his mother's cheek. "Thanks, though. Have fun. I love you."

His parents told Tim they loved him as well before they headed out the door. The lake-house scenario made Tim realize how important his family truly was to him. Being a teenager who had just wanted to get out of the house and get away, Tim had never shown much respect for his parents, but deep down he truly did care for them.

Tim hadn't told his parents he loved them since he turned seventeen, and they couldn't stop smiling as they closed the door behind them. He and Veronica sat on the couch, with Steve relaxing on the recliner because of his legs. They remained quiet as Tim turned on the television. He thought he would not know pain this sharp for a very long time. That was life.

Having to complete high school with two months left would be a tough road. Tim, Veronica, and Steve couldn't imagine themselves walking across the stage without Alan and Richie joining them. But despite all that had taken place, Tim felt closer to everyone around him. He didn't take things for granted anymore—his parents, his friends, or Veronica.

He grasped how much he truly cared for all of them. The three never learned what had happened to the killer's body, once the police escorted them from a bus station they'd managed to get to fifteen minutes after wandering away from Private Property X. It was a perilous task, with Tim having to carry Steve with all his remaining strength, but they made it. Some questions would remain jammed in their minds forever.

"I never thought this would happen," Tim said, breaking the silence.

"No one ever does. No one thinks this stuff will happen to them," Steve replied.

"Because it won't?" Tim asked.

Steve shrugged slightly. But Tim didn't. He became silent once more.

ABOUT THE AUTHOR

J. D. Weisberg studies English with a focus on creative writing at the University of Central Florida. His love of horror films led to his first novel, *The Death Spree*. When he's not writing, Weisberg enjoys training in martial arts and playing bass guitar.

Made in the USA
Columbia, SC
22 December 2018